Enjoy all of these American Girl Mysteries®:

THE SILENT STRANGER A *Kaya* Mystery

LADY MARGARET'S GHOST A *Felicity* Mystery

TRAITOR IN THE SHIPYARD A *Caroline* Mystery

SECRETS IN THE HILLS A *Josefina* Mystery

THE RUNAWAY FRIEND A *Kirsten* Mystery

THE HAUNTED OPERA A *Marie-Grace* Mystery

THE CAMEO NECKLACE A *Cécile* Mystery

SHADOWS ON SOCIETY HILL An *Addy* Mystery

CLUE IN THE CASTLE TOWER A *Samantha* Mystery

THE CRYSTAL BALL A *Rebecca* Mystery

MISSING GRACE A *Kit* Mystery

CLUES IN THE SHADOWS A *Molly* Mystery

THE SILVER GUITAR A *Julie* Mystery

and many more!

— A *Julie* MYSTERY —

LOST IN
THE CITY

by Kathleen O'Dell

★ American Girl®

The Roto-Rooter Plumbing & Drain Service jingle/slogan,
"And Away Go Troubles Down the Drain," is used with
the express permission of Roto-Rooter Group, Inc.

PICTURE CREDITS
The following individuals and organizations have generously
given permission to reprint illustrations contained in "Looking Back":
pp. 136–137—© Niels van Gijn/JAI/Corbis (African Grey parrot);
© KidStock/Blend Images/Corbis (girl holding vegetable basket);
pp. 138–139—courtesy of Mike Lovett (Alex the African Grey parrot);
© Rick Friedman/Corbis (Dr. Irene Pepperberg with Alex); © Lex Hes/
Afripics.com (flock of wild parrots); pp. 140–141—courtesy of Stan Teng (cherry-
headed conures on Telegraph Hill); © iStockphoto.com/alantobey (Coit Tower);
Wild Parrots of Telegraph Hill DVD cover photo © Pelican Media, design by New
Video (*Wild Parrots of Telegraph Hill* film cover); pp. 142–143—jacket cover
copyright © 1977 by Ten Speed Press, a division of Random House, Inc.,
from THE MOOSEWOOD COOKBOOK by Mollie Katzen. Used by
permission of Ten Speed Press, an imprint of the Crown Publishing Group,
a division of Random House, Inc (*Moosewood Cookbook* cover); "Book Cover,"
copyright © 1975 by Ballantine, from DIET FOR A SMALL PLANET
by Frances Moore Lappe. Used by permission of Ballantine Books,
a division of Random House, Inc. (*Diet for a Small Planet* book cover);
courtesy of Lauren Tartaglia and Joshua Walker (Moosewood restaurant
exterior); © KidStock/Blend Images/Corbis (girl holding vegetable basket)

Illustrations by Sergio Giovine

Cataloging-in-Publication Data
available from the Library of Congress

To Elizabeth A. with gratitude

TABLE OF CONTENTS

1

PRETTY BIRD

Julie Albright smiled at the sight of flower boxes bursting with tulips as her father's car made the steep climb up San Francisco's Nob Hill. She couldn't wait to spend her spring break at Dad's house. Ever since her parents' divorce, Julie rarely got to spend more than a weekend with her father, a busy airline pilot. But now, since her older sister, Tracy, was enjoying spring break with her high school friends, Julie would get Dad to herself for the entire week.

Julie turned up the volume on the car radio just in time for the first notes of her favorite new disco song. "Dancing Queen!" she cried, bouncing in her seat. "This song just made number one on the pop charts. Ivy and I can't get enough of it!" Ivy Ling was her best friend and lived across the street from Julie's dad.

Dad laughed. "I hope Ivy is willing to share you this week. Do you think you might be able to spend a day or two with your old dad?"

"Actually," said Julie, "Ivy's going to be gone all week. Her whole family is going to Long Beach for her Uncle Lee's wedding. But I'll get to see her this afternoon before they leave. Did you know the Lings have a new parrot?"

Julie relayed to her dad everything Ivy had told her about the bird. She had belonged to Ivy's Uncle Lee, but he had given her to the Lings a few weeks ago. "Her name is Lucy, and she's an African Grey parrot. Ivy says she's really smart. She talks and sings and even dances! When I was on the phone with Ivy last week, Lucy was imitating a fire-truck siren, and I couldn't believe how real she sounded. Do you think we could get a bird like that?"

Dad looked doubtful. "I think for now we'll stick to being a quiet, one-rabbit family. Nutmeg can't wait to see you," he added.

Julie grinned. She was looking forward

to nuzzling her pet bunny as soon as she got to Dad's house.

When they pulled into the driveway, Julie dashed out of the car and bounded upstairs to her room. "Nutmeg, I'm home!" she called as she swung open her bedroom door. Nutmeg just looked at her and sniffed. "Aw, Nutmeg, I've missed you, too," Julie said. "But you know that pets aren't allowed at Mom's apartment." She gave Nutmeg a gentle snuggle and let the bunny hop around the room while she unpacked.

The telephone rang, and Dad called up the stairs, "It's for you!"

"Hi, Alley-oop," Ivy said when Julie answered. "I just saw your dad's car pull up. Want to come over and meet Lucy?"

"Sure do!" Julie said. "I'll be over soon."

Julie knelt down next to Nutmeg and fed her some kibble from her palm. "Don't worry, Nutmeg. I'll come back and play with you later, I promise." Then she ran downstairs to let Dad know that she was heading over to the Lings'.

"Have fun," Dad said as Julie started out

the door. "But make sure you're home before dinnertime. We have a special visitor coming tonight."

"Ooh!" Julie rubbed her hands together. "Is it a parrot?"

Dad laughed. "Even better than a parrot."

Julie ran across the street and up the stoop to the Lings' front door. Just as she raised her hand to knock, she heard a soft voice. "Hey, um, Albright?"

She squinted at the boy on the sidewalk. "Gordon Marino?" Gordon was the only classmate at her old school who had called her by her last name. But in the two years since she had changed schools, it appeared that he had sprouted almost six inches, and his shaggy blond hair had grown past his shoulders.

"Wow, I almost didn't recognize you!" Julie said, putting her hand up for a high five. He smacked her hand a bit reluctantly and looked down at his shoes. Julie remembered Gordon as the class clown of Sierra Vista School. But now he seemed nervous and shy. "I'm about to go meet Ivy's new talking parrot," she said. "Want to come?"

Gordon's face brightened at her invitation, but then he hesitated. "Do you think Ivy will mind?"

"Gosh, no," said Julie, knocking on the Lings' front door. "Come on!"

Ivy opened the door. "Julie!" she exclaimed, throwing her arms around her friend. Then she looked up. "Hey, Gordon," she said. "Have you come to meet Lucy, the Tap-Dancing Parrot?"

"She can tap-dance, too?" Gordon said, his eyes wide.

"Naw, I'm just fooling with you," Ivy said. Gordon blushed. "But she can do a lot of other amazing things. Come on up. She's in my brother's room with Uncle Lee." She turned and bounced up the stairs with Julie and Gordon close behind her.

When Ivy opened the bedroom door, Julie was surprised to see the large gray parrot standing free on top of her heavy cage, bobbing her head in unison with Ivy's uncle, a man with short black hair who looked about thirty. Julie vaguely remembered seeing him once before, at Ivy's family reunion.

Ivy linked arms with Julie. "Uncle Lee, you remember my best friend, Julie Albright. And this is Gordon Marino, a friend from school."

"Hi, Julie. Nice to meet you, Gordon," said Uncle Lee.

Julie smiled and nodded, but her eyes were locked on the parrot.

"What a cool bird," Gordon murmured.

Uncle Lee chuckled. "I'm guessing you're really here to meet Lucy." He turned to the parrot. "Can you sing for our new friends, Lucy?"

The bird bobbed her neck and wailed, "Call Roto-Rooter, that's the name, and away go troubles down the drain."

Julie had to laugh. "Why the Roto-Rooter theme song?"

"She learned it from the radio," Uncle Lee said, feeding Lucy a chunk of banana. "I've tried to teach her 'Boogie Fever,' but this parrot prefers plumbing to disco, I guess." He smoothed the feathers on Lucy's head.

Julie stepped closer. She had seen parakeets before in pet stores but had never gotten to see an exotic parrot up close. Lucy tilted her head from side to side as she inspected Julie's face. "She looks so intelligent," Julie said. "I wonder what she's thinking." She admired Lucy's silvery body and bright red tail feathers. "And she's such a pretty bird," Julie said.

"Pretty bird! Pretty bird!" Lucy repeated. Everybody laughed, including Gordon. Julie was glad to see that her old friend was starting to loosen up.

Uncle Lee turned to Julie. "I think Lucy likes you. She is usually shy around strangers, but she's really showing off for you today!"

All of a sudden, Lucy started growling and flapping her wings. Julie felt something furry rubbing against her leg.

"Wonton, how did you get in here?" Ivy asked, picking up the orange cat just as it leaped onto the windowsill. "Silly cat! You aren't supposed to be in Andrew's room now that Lucy lives in here."

"Silly cat!" Lucy repeated, strutting across the top of her cage and glaring at the cat in Ivy's arms.

Uncle Lee reached up, and the parrot stepped onto his arm. "African Grey parrots are extra sensitive. She's used to living alone with me. Moving to a house full of people and cats has been a bit of a shock to her."

Ivy scratched behind the cat's ears. "And I don't think Jasmine and Wonton are too happy with the change, either. They used to love sitting on Andrew's windowsill to catch the sun in the afternoon. Now that he has to keep his door closed, I think they feel rejected."

Uncle Lee stroked Lucy's feathers to calm her as Ivy shooed the cat out the door. "I'm sure the cats can find a place to get their sun somewhere else," he said. "Now, who wants to see Lucy do some more tricks?"

Gordon piped up. "I do!"

Uncle Lee winked at Ivy. "Ivy and I have been working on teaching her a couple of things."

Ivy grinned and turned to the parrot on

Uncle Lee's arm. She held up a chunk of banana and said, "Lucy, say hello to Julie."

"Hey, Alley-oop!" the parrot squawked. Ivy giggled and fed the bird the banana.

"You taught her my nickname?" Julie squealed. Ivy beamed and nodded. "But how did she learn it?"

"It took some practice," Ivy said. She explained how she and Uncle Lee worked together to teach her. Lucy would watch as Ivy said "Julie" and held up the piece of banana in her hand. When Uncle Lee said, "Hey, Alley-oop," Ivy would give him the banana. After a while, Lucy started mimicking his words to earn the treat herself.

"Wow," said Julie. "That's amazing. I wish I could teach my bunny to do that!"

Julie and Gordon laughed as Lucy, Ivy, and Uncle Lee put on a show for them. Ivy had taught Lucy to dance across the top of her cage whenever she sang the chorus to "Dancing Queen." Uncle Lee flapped his elbows like a chicken, and Lucy responded with a screeching cock-a-doodle-doo. For the finale, Lucy performed her famous fire-truck siren impression, earning herself another piece of banana.

Julie and Gordon gave a round of applause as Uncle Lee, Ivy, and even Lucy bowed.

"Bravo!" said Julie. "Uncle Lee, do you think Lucy would let me hold her?"

Uncle Lee pursed his lips. "Well, it usually takes Lucy a while to grow comfortable with strangers—but you could try."

Uncle Lee guided Julie's arm up to where Lucy was standing on top of her cage. Julie's heart skipped a beat as the parrot stepped onto her forearm. Glowing, she lowered Lucy down and, with her free hand, gently stroked the silvery feathers on the back of her head.

Uncle Lee grinned. "She really feels comfortable around you, I can tell."

"What a pretty bird," Julie crooned to the parrot. "Do you like me, Lucy? Julie likes you."

"Pretty bird. Alley-oop!" Lucy replied, cocking her head and gazing into Julie's face.

Julie laughed with delight. "You're so lucky,

Ivy. I wish I had a parrot like Lucy."

"Once we're back from Long Beach, you can visit any time you'd like," said Ivy.

Julie noticed that the sun was low in the sky and realized that it was time to say good-bye and go home for dinner. She raised her arm to return Lucy to the top of the cage.

"I'm going to miss you while you're gone," Julie said as she gave Ivy a tight squeeze.

"I'll be back next Saturday," Ivy said. "Won't that be your last day at your dad's? We can hang out then."

Julie nodded and turned to Uncle Lee, who was leaning toward the cage so that Lucy could hop down onto his shoulder. "It was nice to see you, Uncle Lee. You too, Lucy. Good-bye!"

"Good-bye!" Lucy squawked, bobbing her head for Julie.

Gordon gave a timid wave to Ivy and Uncle Lee and followed Julie down the stairs and out the door. "Man," said Gordon. "I couldn't believe all the tricks Lucy could do. She should be on TV or something!"

"I know," said Julie. "That was *so* much fun. I wish the Lings were going to be here this week so that we could visit some more."

Gordon kicked his toe against the sidewalk. "It's a bummer that you won't get to hang out with Ivy this week, but I'll be around if you get bored at your dad's house," he said. "I moved just down the street last month, to that green house. The one with the white trim."

Julie nodded. "I know that one."

"Yeah . . . well, anyway, if you don't want to hang out, that's okay." He looked down at his feet.

"Of course we can hang out. We could go shoot some hoops at the park."

Gordon brightened. "Sounds cool. Guess I'll see you later, Albright." He turned and started walking toward his house.

As Julie watched him shuffle down the sidewalk, she wondered why he seemed so glum. *He used to be such a clown,* she thought, remembering how he would cross his eyes and do backflips on the playground to make people laugh. She shrugged and headed back home.

Just as she reached her front walk, she heard Ivy call, "Alley-oop! Wait up!" Ivy darted across the empty street and put her hands on Julie's shoulders. "I have a big favor to ask."

"Anything for you," Julie replied.

"Well, it's really for Uncle Lee. He was so impressed with the way you and Lucy hit it off that he wants to cancel the pet sitter we lined up for the week—and hire you."

Julie felt her face warm. "Me? Really?"

"He's super protective of Lucy. He still thinks of her as—well, as his baby. But Hannah, his fiancée, refuses to live in the same house with a parrot—she says they're too noisy—so that's why he gave her to us. Uncle Lee hardly even trusts *us* with Lucy yet, but he says that you really had a special connection with her." Ivy hesitated. "Do you think you could do it?"

Julie felt a rush of excitement. A whole week with the smartest bird in the world! "I'd love to!" Julie said.

"Thank you so much," Ivy said, looking relieved. "You have no idea what this means to Uncle Lee. And I know you'll take great care of her while we're gone."

Julie beamed at the compliment. She was overwhelmed with pride that Uncle Lee would choose her to take care of his beloved parrot. Julie hoped that Uncle Lee and Ivy were right about her special connection with Lucy. She would certainly do her very best to take good care of the bird.

2

A Special Guest

Ivy handed Julie a sheet of paper and a macramé key chain holding a single key. "Here are some instructions for taking care of Lucy that Uncle Lee wrote up, and here's a key to our house," she said.

Julie turned over the page and gulped as she saw that the directions continued on the back side. How would she ever remember everything on this list?

"I'm sorry it's so long," Ivy said. "Uncle Lee just wants to make sure you're prepared for any situation. But if you have any questions, we also wrote down the phone numbers for the vet and our hotel just in case. We're leaving super early tomorrow, so would you mind coming by in the morning to feed Lucy and the cats?"

"Sure, I don't mind," Julie said. She took a deep breath and raised her right hand. "I hereby promise to be the best parrot sitter in all of human history."

"You will be, no doubt about it!" said Ivy. "Oh, one more thing: we have an elderly couple, Mr. and Mrs. Shackley, staying downstairs for the next week. They're the parents of one of my mom's law-school classmates. Mrs. Shackley just received a kidney transplant, and she and her husband needed a place closer to the hospital to rest after the surgery." She went on to explain that the Lings had shut the pocket door that led from the entryway into the living room to give the couple some privacy. The Shackleys would use the living room, dining room, and kitchen as their temporary living space, while the entryway and the stairwell would remain free for Julie to come and go to the floors above. "You probably won't be seeing much of the Shackleys," Ivy continued. "They keep pretty much to themselves."

"I'll be fine," Julie said, giving Ivy one more hug.

A SPECIAL GUEST

As Julie waved good-bye to her friend, a taxi pulled up to the curb. Out stepped a wild-haired young woman weighed down with duffel bags and groceries. She was wearing bell-bottom jeans, a flowered peasant shirt, and a dazzling smile.

"Aunt Maia!" Julie squealed.

Maia set down her bags and threw open her arms for a hug. "So good to see you, Julie! How's my niece? Still a little rabble-rouser, I hope? Cleaning up oil spills and saving the California condor?"

"Actually, it wasn't condors I was saving—it was a family of bald eagles." Julie smiled. "I raised money to release them back into the wild."

Maia grinned. "Don't tell your father, but I think you take after me."

Julie grabbed her aunt's heavy canvas bags and led Maia up the front stoop. Julie's dad opened the front door. "Well, I see you've found our special guest. Mary made me keep her plans to visit a surprise."

"Dad, she goes by Maia now," Julie said.

Dad winced. "Still getting used to the name change, I guess. She was Mary to me for twenty-something years, so both you and Maia will have to forgive me if I slip."

"Oh, Dan—still the same big brother, I see," said Maia with a laugh.

Julie could remember years ago when Dad's sister "Maia" was "Aunt Mary"—a shy, serious college student. After a few years of college, she had undergone a transformation. Julie was inspired by her aunt's courage to reinvent herself as Maia, an outspoken young woman who wanted to save the planet.

Aunt Maia peered into her grocery bags. "Let's get this stuff into the house before it wilts."

As Dad scooped up grocery bags brimming with vegetables, Julie squirmed under the weight of Maia's luggage. "Gosh, Aunt Maia, how long are you going to be staying?" she asked.

"Tired of me already?" Maia smiled. "Actually, I'm moving to San Francisco. Your dad was nice enough to let me stay here until I can find a place of my own."

"Stay as long as you'd like," said Dad. "It gets lonely around here without my girls." He ruffled Julie's blonde hair.

"So, we get to hang out together all week?" Julie asked Maia. This was turning into the best spring break ever!

"Sorry, sweetie, not quite. I took a job as an assistant chef at a new vegetarian restaurant. I start on Monday, so it's going to be a very busy week for me. But we'll catch up tonight. In fact, I have a special dinner planned for you and your dad. You can preview my favorite dishes and even a couple of new recipes that I'm trying out."

"Yay!" Julie cried. She remembered that Aunt Maia made great lasagna. Her mouth was watering already.

Once Julie and Maia were done carrying Maia's bags up to Tracy's room, they went down to the kitchen to prepare dinner. Julie surveyed the ingredients Maia spread over the kitchen counter. Some of the foods Julie recognized: carrots, onions, and tomatoes. But there was also a bundle of bushy, purplish leafy greens and something dried, dark green, and fishy-smelling that almost made Julie sneeze. Then there was a block of slimy-looking white stuff, some orange paste, and a bowlful of grains.

"Uh, Aunt Maia?" Julie said. "Aren't we missing something?"

Maia looked over the spread. "Nope. Don't think so. Everything's here."

"But where's the meat? Mom always makes us chicken or pork chops or something."

"I'm a vegetarian now, Julie. That means I don't eat meat."

Julie tried to imagine what it would be like to be a vegetarian. She liked salads and macaroni and cheese a lot. But she wasn't sure she could ever live without hamburgers or the yummy sesame chicken from The Happy Panda, Ivy's grandparents' restaurant.

Julie picked up a purple leaf and examined it. "Mom always says that growing girls need their protein."

"We've got protein right here," Maia said,

pointing her spoon at the slimy white stuff. "This is called tofu. It's made from soybeans."

"Oh, yeah," Julie said. "I think I've had tofu before, in Chinese food. Ivy's mom calls it bean curd."

Julie was pleasantly surprised when they sat down to eat. She loved the spiced carrot-and-lentil salad and the miso soup with silky cubes of tofu, bits of seaweed, and green onion. But she couldn't quite bring herself to taste the fishy-smelling greens that Maia had piled on her plate. Dad hadn't touched his either.

"Just try one bite, Dan," Maia said to Julie's dad. "It's a new recipe that I'm trying out for the restaurant, and I need to know what you think. A little raw kale with seaweed dressing isn't going to kill you. Here, I'll go first."

Maia scooped a huge forkful of the greens into her mouth and turned bright red almost immediately. Julie and Dad tried to stifle their giggles when Maia finally choked down the mouthful with a shiver.

"Blech! I guess I'm glad I tried this recipe

21

before I humiliated myself on my first day at the restaurant," Maia said.

Once all the dishes were clean, Julie rinsed the raw kale and went upstairs to feed some of it to Nutmeg. "Aunt Maia will be happy this isn't going to waste," Julie told Nutmeg as the rabbit munched away. "She hasn't seen you since you were a baby bunny. Would you like to see her?" Nutmeg wiggled her nose. "I'll take that as a yes." Julie knew that her aunt was a real animal lover and that she'd adore Nutmeg. Suddenly Julie had another great idea: maybe Maia would like to come with her to the Lings' tomorrow to meet Lucy!

Julie picked up the rabbit and brought her downstairs. "Say hello to Aunt Maia, Nutmeg," Julie said, waving the bunny's paw in her aunt's direction.

"Well, hello, Nutmeg. How nice to see you all grown up! Julie, do you think your bunny would like to hop around a bit and stretch her legs?"

Julie set Nutmeg on the floor. At first the rabbit just sat there and sniffed the carpet. But when Dad came into the room, Nutmeg got startled and began hopping wildly about the living room, picking up speed as she approached the kitchen.

"Stop her, Dad!" cried Julie.

Maia leaped up to head off the rabbit, knocking over a chair. Dad lunged forward and reached for Nutmeg like a baseball player diving for home base. "I've got her!" he yelled. But Nutmeg simply reversed direction and hopped over him into the kitchen.

Julie ducked under the kitchen table, ready to intercept as the frantic rabbit skimmed over the floor and glided into her arms.

Dad's hands shot up. "Goal!" he shouted.

"Three points!" hollered Maia, flushed and grinning.

Julie held the quivering rabbit close and felt Nutmeg's heart banging against her ribs. "Hey there, little bunny, what's gotten into you?"

"I think she got spooked," Maia said.

Julie frowned. "By Dad? But she knows him."

"She's used to him when she's in your familiar

room, but this is strange territory to her," said Maia. "She wouldn't scare so easily if you'd let her explore the house more. In fact, she would be a much happier rabbit if she was allowed to hop freely from room to room. Rabbits can be litter-box trained, you know. If you trained Nutmeg, she wouldn't have to be in a cage at all."

Dad shook his head. "Sorry, Nutmeg. I don't think that's going to happen."

Julie looked at Nutmeg. Except for this little scare, she didn't seem to be unhappy. Julie knew that Dad sometimes let her run around a bit when he was home, and Ivy often came over to give her some exercise whenever Dad was out of town for work. Julie wondered what Maia would think about a parrot being cooped up in a cage.

3
A Troubling Visit

The next morning, Julie found her dad in the kitchen making breakfast.

"Who wants flapjacks and bacon?" Dad asked. He flipped a pancake into the air and caught it in the skillet. Julie applauded as Dad gave an exaggerated bow.

"I do!" Julie said. "But I doubt Aunt Maia will want any of that bacon when she comes down to eat."

"Mary—er, Maia left already. She said she wanted to explore the neighborhood around her new restaurant to see if she could find an apartment to rent."

Julie slumped in her chair. "Shoot, I was going to bring Aunt Maia to the Lings' to meet Lucy. Maybe tomorrow?"

"Tomorrow she'll be training at the restaurant in preparation for her new job." Dad slid a plate of steaming flapjacks with butter and syrup under Julie's nose. "Don't worry, you'll get to see her tonight. She'll be back in time to cook us another dinner." Dad grinned, and then he leaned down and whispered in her ear, "So you'd better fill up on some seaweed-free breakfast now!"

Julie scarfed down enough pancakes and slices of bacon to make her belly ache. "Thanks for breakfast, Dad. I'm stuffed! Now I've got to go feed Lucy and the cats."

Julie grabbed the macramé key chain from the ceramic bowl Dad kept in the foyer and went across the street. Inside the Lings' front hall, Julie found Jasmine, the gray cat, pawing at the closed pocket door that led to the rooms where the Shackleys were staying.

Julie scooped up the cat. "Oh, Jasmine, leave the Shackleys alone. Come on, let's go upstairs. I'll feed you as soon as I'm done feeding Lucy."

Julie dropped Jasmine at the top of the stairs and walked down the hall to Andrew's room, surprised at how warm the house was. The Shackleys must have set the thermostat extra high, Julie thought. At Andrew's door, she peeked in and called, "Lucy, say hello to Julie!"

She closed the bedroom door behind her and approached the cage, which was covered by a white sheet. Julie remembered that Uncle Lee's instructions had said to cover the cage with the white sheet at night to calm Lucy and help her sleep. "Wake up, sleepyhead!" she said softly. She pulled the sheet off the cage and gasped. The bird was motionless, curled in a gray lump on her perch. Julie tapped on the cage and watched the parrot unfold like origami. Lucy had only been sleeping with her head under her wing.

"Thank goodness," Julie said. "Whew, it's stuffy in here. Let's give you some fresh air." Andrew's window sprang open when she pushed the latch, and she stuck her head out the window to take in the eucalyptus-scented breeze.

She turned back to Lucy, who looked at her with bright yellow eyes. "Can you show me your dance?" Julie asked, bobbing her head as Uncle Lee had yesterday. Lucy blinked at her but didn't move. "How about we try a song then?" Julie suggested. "Call Roto-Rooter, that's the name . . ." She waited for Lucy to finish the line, but instead the parrot inched away from Julie on her perch.

"What's wrong, Lucy? Aren't you feeling well? I know, you're probably hungry."

Julie pulled out Uncle Lee's instructions and followed them carefully. She filled Lucy's bowl with seeds and broke up a banana onto a plate inside the cage. Lucy ignored the food and turned her back to stare out the window. Julie frowned, wondering why Lucy seemed so down. She flashed back to Maia's comment that Nutmeg would be happier if she could hop freely around the house. Clearly Lucy was used to being out of her cage with Uncle Lee. Would Lucy be happier if she was out of her cage? Then Julie remembered Uncle Lee's directions that said she should wait a couple of days before letting Lucy out, so that the parrot could get used to Julie's presence. "I'm sorry, Lucy," she said.

"I promise to let you out as soon as I can."

Julie decided to leave the parrot to eat in peace. As soon as she closed the door behind her, Jasmine and Wonton began rubbing against her legs and purring in anticipation of being fed. "I'm glad *someone's* happy to see me," Julie told them.

She remembered something else that Uncle Lee had said yesterday: Lucy usually didn't like strangers. Julie felt a heaviness in her stomach. Could Uncle Lee have been wrong about the parrot's connection with Julie? *What if Lucy doesn't like me*, Julie thought, *and the Lings come back to a different, sad bird?* Still worried by this notion, Julie picked up the new bag of kibble that Ivy had left next to the cats' bowls in her room. She pulled the tab at the top of the bag, and the bag burst open, sending little brown pellets scattering across the floor.

"Way to go, Julie!" she scolded herself. She quickly filled the bowls and then swept up the spilled kibble. Leaving the cats eating their breakfast, she returned to Andrew's room. She was glad to see that Lucy had eaten some banana and was now pecking at the seeds in her bowl.

"I'll come back to see you this afternoon, Lucy. Maybe then I can find a way to cheer you up." She locked the birdcage gate with the safety clip and shut Andrew's bedroom window before closing the bedroom door.

She thumped down the stairs and was almost out the front door when she heard the pocket door slide open. Julie turned and saw an old man peeking through the crack in the doorway. "Mr. Shackley?" she said, putting on a friendly smile.

The man slid the door open a little wider. "Who are you, and what are you doing here?" he rasped.

"I'm Julie Albright, the Lings' pet sitter."

Mr. Shackley let out a shaky breath. "All that noise! I knew a pet sitter was coming, but with the ruckus, I thought it must be a prowler. And my poor wife!"

"I'm so sorry," Julie said. "I spilled the cat food by mistake. I'll be more quiet next time, I promise."

"Please do that, my dear," he said. "My wife can take no excitement, you see. No noise at all! And I haven't had a full night's sleep since my wife's surgery. Puts a man out of sorts."

Julie nodded. "I'm sorry," she said again.

"If I had my way, we'd have hauled ourselves back to Laytonville as soon as she was discharged. But it's too long a drive, and my son insisted we stay here in the city, near the hospital." He wrung his hands. "This city has frayed my last nerve. The noise, the traffic! Don't know how anyone can stand it."

"It's not so bad, really," Julie said, "once you get used to it."

"I could never get used to it," he said curtly. "And please mind how you climb these stairs. Girls these days walk like lumberjacks. Now, if you'll excuse me . . . "

Julie stood mute as he slid the door shut without saying good-bye. As quietly as she could, she locked the front door, stepped down to the sidewalk, and watched Mr. Shackley draw the draperies tight across the front windows.

4
THE WHITE SHEET

That afternoon, Julie sat on the front stoop and stared at Ivy's house across the street, mulling over the responsibility she had taken on. She knew that she could brighten Nutmeg's mood by giving her carrots and broccoli, but what could she do to give a lift to an unhappy parrot?

Julie was so lost in her thoughts that she didn't notice Gordon until he was standing right in front of her. "Hey, Albright," he said, his eyes following the direction of her gaze. He sat down next to her. "What's up? You missing Ivy?"

"Hi, Gordon. Just thinking about Lucy. I'm pet-setting for her while the Lings are in Long Beach. But when I visited her this morning, she didn't seem very happy."

"Maybe she's lonely," Gordon murmured.

"I know the feeling." He stuffed his hands in the pockets of his shabby old San Francisco Giants jacket. Julie noticed that his fingers were poking out of the pocket linings and resting on his thighs.

"Air-conditioning," he said, wiggling his fingers.

Julie smiled. "Must be an old favorite."

"Not really," he said. "But I lost my good jacket, the one I got for my birthday last month, and my mom thinks she's teaching me responsibility by making me wear this one until I earn the money for a replacement." Gordon sighed, looking glum. "At this rate, it will be a whole year before I can afford a new one."

Julie tried to think of a way to cheer up her old friend. Then she had an idea. "How would you like to come with me to visit Ivy's parrot?"

A smile spread across Gordon's face. "Sure!"

Julie was pleased to see Gordon perk up. *Maybe his good mood will rub off on Lucy*, she hoped as she led him across the street.

"You think Lucy will remember me?" Gordon asked.

"I don't think she'd forget you after one day," Julie told him. "Parrots are very smart."

When Julie opened the door, Gordon jumped ahead and called out, "Last one up's a rotten egg!"

"Shhh!" Julie winced, expecting Mr. Shackley to slide open the pocket door and scold her once again. But she didn't hear any shuffling behind the door. "There's an elderly couple staying on the bottom floor of the Lings' house," she whispered. "I already got in trouble with the man this morning for making too much noise. But it looks as if maybe they're not home."

Still, Julie and Gordon were careful to tiptoe up the stairs, just in case. Julie gripped the knob on the bedroom door and in a loud whisper announced, "Heeeere's Lucy!" She swung open the door—and stopped in her tracks. The cage was covered with a white sheet.

"That's strange," Julie murmured. "Ivy's instructions said to cover Lucy's cage at night. But I took the sheet off the cage when I visited Lucy this morning, and I didn't put it back on when I left." She paused, frowning. "Gordon, somebody has been in here."

Julie stepped up to the cage, grabbed a corner of the sheet, and lifted the sheet off the cage. To her relief, she found Lucy standing on her perch, as bright-eyed and alert as she had been the day before.

"Thank goodness she's okay." She went to the window and popped open the lock to let in some fresh air.

Gordon followed her and stuck his head out the window. "Whoa, there's a fire escape out here!" he said. "You ever go out on this thing?"

"Naw. Mrs. Ling says it's for emergencies only."

"Too bad," Gordon said. He took off his jacket and dropped it on the bed before approaching Lucy's cage.

Lucy danced back and forth across her perch. When Gordon flapped his elbows, Lucy crowed. "Cock-a-doodle-doo!"

"She remembers me!" Gordon said.

"See? I told you." Julie was relieved that Lucy was back to her old self. Still, she couldn't help feeling a little jealous that it seemed to be

Gordon who had made the difference in the bird's mood. Maybe Uncle Lee had been mistaken about Julie's connection with Lucy— maybe *Gordon* was the one Lucy had actually responded to! But her worries didn't last long.

"Hi, Lucy," Julie said. "Do you remember me? Can you say hello to Julie?" She peeled a banana and broke off a chunk.

"Hey, Alley-oop!" Lucy said, bobbing her head in Julie's direction.

Julie smiled and gave Lucy the banana. "You've had quite a day, haven't you. Can you tell me who covered your cage?"

"Pretty bird!" Lucy squawked.

Gordon chuckled. "I don't think we're going to get any answers out of her. But we might get a song. Can you sing for us, Lucy?"

As the parrot belted out the Roto-Rooter theme song, Julie watched Gordon break into a grin. "Gordon, do you want to come with me to visit Lucy again this week?" Julie asked.

"Definitely!" he said. He looked down at his shoes. "I've always wanted to have a bird like

Lucy to keep me company at home, but my mom won't let me have any pets."

Julie shook her head in sympathy, thinking about how much she missed Nutmeg whenever she was at her mom's apartment, which was most of the time.

Gordon looked at the clock on Andrew's desk. "Speaking of my mom, she's expecting me to be home for dinner soon. I should get going."

Julie nodded. "Okay, Lucy. I'll be back to visit tomorrow." She draped the sheet over the cage.

"Good night, Lucy," said Gordon.

Julie checked the room for stowaway cats. As she closed the bedroom door behind Gordon, he turned to her. "Hey, Julie? Do you think Lucy might be lonely being all by herself in that room? Couldn't you keep her at your house so she has company?"

"Uncle Lee says that it's important for Lucy to get used to her new environment. So we'll just have to visit her a lot this week."

"Sounds good to me," Gordon said. They were halfway down the stairs when Gordon screeched to a halt. "Oh, I forgot my jacket upstairs! What would my mom say if I lost that one, too?"

Julie waited by the front door as he ran back up to Andrew's room and hustled down the stairs moments later with the jacket over his arm. "Hey, Gordon, do you want to come over and meet my Aunt Maia?" she asked, opening the door.

Gordon bit the inside of his cheek, looking nervous. "Um, I'd better get home. My mom will be mad if I'm not home in time for dinner." He dashed past her. "See you tomorrow," he called over his shoulder.

When she returned home, Julie dropped her key into the bowl and found Dad in the kitchen keeping Maia company while she made dinner. "Hey, kiddo," he greeted her. "How was your first day of bird-sitting?"

"Actually, it was kind of strange." She dropped into her chair and told Dad and Maia about the mysterious appearance of the white sheet. "Nothing else was out of place," Julie assured Dad. "Except for that sheet."

"That's odd," Maia said. "Do you know of anyone who has a key to the house?"

"Well, I have a key, but I keep it here, in the bowl in the foyer. I have no idea if they gave a key to anyone else. Of course, there are the Shackleys," said Julie, explaining about the Lings' temporary houseguests. "But Mrs. Shackley is recovering from surgery, and Mr. Shackley is very busy taking care of her, so I don't think it was them. I mean, that's why Ivy's family hired someone else to take care of the animals— otherwise the Shackleys could have done it."

Julie went on to explain that Lucy had been acting unusually quiet that morning and that she had been worried about the bird until she and Gordon visited that afternoon.

"Maybe you should let Lucy out of her cage the next time you visit," Maia said. "I would be depressed, too, if I were cooped up in a cage all the time." She placed the last steaming dish on the table and sat down. "Dig in!"

Julie turned to Maia. "Uncle Lee said I should

keep Lucy in the cage for the first couple of days that the Lings are away," Julie explained. "He said it was important for her to adjust to her new life without him at Ivy's house. I don't want anything bad to happen if I don't follow his directions."

Maia raised a critical eyebrow before picking up a forkful of sautéed tofu. "Guess you've got to do what you've got to do."

Maia took a small bite, frowned, and let the fork fall back onto her plate. "You know, I'm not feeling very hungry. If you don't mind, I'm going to excuse myself and go get some fresh air." She pushed away from the table, grabbed a key from the bowl in the foyer, and closed the front door behind her.

"I wonder what got into her," Dad said.

He and Julie each took a bite. "I think I know," Julie said, her eyes watering as she choked down the overspiced tofu.

5
MISSING!

The next morning, Julie ran to Maia's room to wish her good luck for her training day at work, but she was disappointed to find that her aunt had already left. Julie went down to the kitchen, popped some bread into the toaster for breakfast, and ate quickly, eager to go visit Lucy. It was probably too early to call Gordon to see if he would want to come with her, so Julie went alone to the foyer and reached into the bowl for the macramé key chain. When she peered into the bowl and stirred around, though, she found nothing but Dad's keys, a shoelace, and a crumpled receipt.

Dad wandered down the stairs in his bathrobe. He yawned. "Morning, Julie. You're up early."

"I wanted to check on Lucy first thing this

morning, but I can't find the Lings' house key. I'm sure I put it in the bowl. Have you seen it?"

Mr. Albright helped look around the foyer. "Here it is. It was right next to the bowl, under Maia's scarf," he said, gathering the length of blue silk from where Maia had dropped it.

"Oh, good—thanks so much!" Julie said, hugging Dad. "When I get back, do you want to have a father-daughter day?"

"I'd love that. We could play Frisbee in Golden Gate Park. I'll be ready for you when you're done feeding the animals."

Inside the front hall at Ivy's house, Julie hesitated. Should she ask Mr. Shackley whether he had covered the cage? Summoning her courage, she knocked softly on the pocket door, but nobody answered. Perhaps they were still sleeping. Julie decided that she'd come back with Dad on their way home from the park.

As Julie tiptoed quietly up the stairs, she smelled the familiar outdoor scent of eucalyptus leaves. Suddenly she felt a prickle on the back of her neck. Something wasn't right.

MISSING!

She turned toward Andrew's room and caught her breath. The bedroom door was ajar. Had someone gone into the room again? She hurried down the hall and into the room, where she surveyed the scene before her as if in a dream. The gate to Lucy's cage was hanging open, and Lucy was nowhere to be seen. The white sheet was in a crumpled pile on the floor next to the cage's safety clip. Julie picked both of them up off the floor and placed them on Andrew's desk.

She looked up and felt her heart drop. The window was open. She rushed over and scanned the surrounding tree branches and the roof of the apartment building across the alley, but there was no sign of Lucy. Then she heard a meow coming from the fire escape.

"Oh my gosh, Wonton!" She climbed out the window and picked up the cat. "What are you doing out here? And where's Jasmine?"

Julie ducked back into Andrew's room and closed the window. She set Wonton down in the hallway and ran from room to room. "Lucy? Jasmine?" she called as she checked under Ivy's parents' bed and behind the curtains. Wonton padded into the room and gave a plaintive meow. "I know, Wonton," Julie said. "I'm scared, too."

She dashed into the bathroom and checked the tub and between the shower curtains. She even looked inside the closed cabinets and in the laundry basket. She ran to the next room and found Jasmine lounging on Ivy's bed. "There you are, Jasmine! Thank goodness you're safe."

But where was Lucy? Julie looked everywhere a parrot could hide in Ivy's room, and then she slumped down on the edge of the bed next to Jasmine. Could the cats have gotten Lucy? She quickly shook away the thought. After all, there were no feathers anywhere, and the open window in Andrew's room certainly suggested that Lucy had flown away. A tear streamed down Julie's cheek, and she felt something heavy in the pit of her stomach. Lucy was gone.

She filled the cats' bowls and left, questions flooding her mind. Where could Lucy be? Was she safe? How would they ever find her? Julie burst through the front door of her house, out of breath and on the verge of panic.

Dad looked up from his newspaper. "Ready to go—hey, kiddo, what's wrong?"

Julie tearfully explained her discovery: the open door, the empty cage and open window, the sheet and clip on the floor. "But Dad, I *know* I closed the bedroom door and the window yesterday. I'm sure of it!"

Dad pulled Julie into a hug. "I believe you, sweetheart. From what I can tell, this isn't your fault."

"Do you think we should call the police?" Julie asked.

Dad thought for a moment and then asked, "When you were in the house, did you see any signs of a break-in, like a broken window? Was anything else missing?"

"No, everything else seemed to be in the right place."

"Well, that's a relief. However, I don't think the police will respond to a report of a missing pet unless there are signs of a break-in or burglary. But we are going to have to let the Lings know what has happened right away."

Julie cringed. How would Ivy react when Julie broke the news? Would she ever be able to trust Julie again? "Oh, Dad, I—I don't know if I can."

Dad gave her a reassuring squeeze. "Now, honey, since Lucy was your responsibility—and because you're the one who made the discovery—I think you should be the one who makes the phone call. Remember, it doesn't mean her disappearance is your fault."

Julie nodded bravely. She dialed the number of Ivy's hotel and asked for Ivy's parents' room. To her relief, Ivy answered the phone.

"Hi, Alley-oop," Ivy said. "Things have been crazy around here!"

"Here, too." Julie looked at her dad, who gave her a reassuring nod. She started in. "Listen, Ivy—"

But before she could explain about Lucy, Ivy broke in. "Guess what—you'll never believe it. Uncle Lee is gone!"

"What do you mean? I thought he was getting married! Did he . . . did he change his mind?"

"We're not sure," Ivy said. "He disappeared sometime between last night and this morning, and no one knows where he is. We think he may be upset about Lucy."

"Lucy?" Julie gulped. How could Uncle Lee and the Lings already know that Lucy was missing when Julie had only just made the discovery herself?

"He left a note behind for Hannah, his fiancée. It said that she's asking him to make too many sacrifices for the marriage, and he needs some time to think things over. He didn't mention Lucy in particular, but we all think that he's most upset about giving her up. He's had that parrot since he was eighteen." Ivy sighed into the phone. "Hannah was over here sobbing this morning. I feel so bad for her. She says that what she adores most about Uncle Lee is that he's so loving, and she should have known how much giving up Lucy would hurt him."

That's when Julie had an idea. "Ivy, I think maybe I know where Uncle Lee went."

"You do? Where?"

"I think he came back to San Francisco to get Lucy!" Julie explained the discovery she had made this morning.

For a few moments there was silence on the line. Then Ivy said, "But he doesn't have a key to our house."

"Then he must have gotten in through the fire escape. It goes right to Andrew's window. That would explain why the window was open."

"Gee, I sure hope you're right," Ivy said, sounding uncertain. "I mean, the wedding is supposed to take place this afternoon. Let's hope he comes back—with Lucy."

They were both quiet for a moment, and Julie felt her confidence leaking away. Could Uncle Lee have taken a plane to San Francisco last night? Why wouldn't he have let her know that he was taking Lucy back? Well, maybe because he didn't want anyone to know where he was if he was ducking out on his wedding, Julie thought ruefully. But still, wouldn't he have at least taken Lucy's cage? *Perhaps he doesn't need it because he knows Lucy won't leave him,* Julie realized. Besides, the cage wouldn't fit through Andrew's window.

"Ivy," Julie said, "I won't stop looking for Lucy. And if I find out anything more, I'll call you right away."

"Thanks, Julie," said Ivy. "And I'll call you if I hear anything about Uncle Lee."

6
PARROT PURSUIT

Julie hung up and told Dad the news about Uncle Lee's sudden departure and her theory that it was related to Lucy's disappearance.

Dad looked thoughtful. "It's certainly possible that Lucy is with Uncle Lee, but just to be safe, I think we should call the Humane Society to see if anyone has found her and turned her in."

"Great idea," Julie said. She thumbed through the phone book and dialed the number for the Humane Society. "Hello, I'd like to report a missing bird, an African Grey parrot named Lucy. She has a gray body, a bright red tail, a black beak, and a white ring around each eye. Has anybody turned in a bird like that?"

"I'm sorry," said the receptionist. "We haven't seen any African Greys. But I'll take your name and phone number. If anyone reports finding or spotting an African Grey parrot, we'll call you right away." Then she added, "I know that losing a pet can make you feel powerless. But one thing you can do is post missing-pet flyers around your neighborhood to spread the word."

Julie thanked her for the suggestion, gave her contact information, and hung up feeling a little more hopeful. "Dad, instead of going to the park today, would you help me put up missing-pet flyers around town?"

"You bet," Dad said. "Why don't you draw up a poster, and I'll take it to the library to make copies. We'll have to cover a wide area—our missing pet has wings. Maybe you could call a friend to help."

Julie nodded. "I'll call Gordon. He'll be so sad when he hears that Lucy's missing. He really likes her."

"Here," Dad said, pulling a list of community numbers from under a magnet on the refrigerator. "Just dial the number for the North Beach Neigh-borhood Committee. It's the Marinos' home phone. Gordon's mom heads the committee."

Julie dialed the number, and Gordon answered. "Hey, Albright—is it parrot-feeding time?"

"Gordon, I hate to tell you this," Julie began. She told him everything that had happened and asked if he would help her post flyers.

"Man, that's terrible," Gordon said. "I want to help, but there's something I need to do first. My dad could drive me over in about an hour, if that's okay?"

"That's fine," said Julie. "I still need to draw the missing poster, and my dad has to make copies at the library."

After hanging up the phone, Julie gathered paper, markers, and pencils. She paged through the encyclopedia and found a picture of a parrot to copy.

At the top of the page, she wrote "MISSING!" in big, bold letters. Then she drew a large parrot in pencil, being careful to shade the belly a little lighter than the back and leaving white rings around her eyes. Underneath she wrote Lucy's name and described a couple of her best tricks:

singing the Roto-Rooter theme song and imitating a fire-truck siren. Then she wrote the date the bird went missing and Dad's phone number. When she finished, she held up the poster to show her father.

"That looks great, Julie," he said, throwing on a denim jacket. "It's too bad we won't have time to color in the red tail on the photocopies, but I think anyone who sees a parrot flying around will be able to recognize her. I'll be back from the library in a jiffy."

While Dad was still out making copies, the doorbell rang, and Julie opened the door to find Gordon. Instead of his shabby old Giants jacket, he was wearing a beautiful black leather jacket.

"Wow, Gordon, looking smooth! Is this the jacket you lost?"

"Nope," he said, popping up his collar and gliding his fingers down the lapels. "This is the jacket that I was saving up for. I just got it this morning. Look, there are even zippers on the sleeves!" He showed her a wrist and coolly slid the zipper pull up and down.

Julie was confused. Hadn't Gordon said just yesterday that he wouldn't be able to afford a new jacket for a year? "How did you manage to save up all the money in one day?" she asked.

Gordon blushed. "I—well, you see . . ." he stammered. But before he could explain, Mr. Albright trotted up the sidewalk with a thick pile of flyers in his hands. "Hey there, Gordon. Nice jacket. You kids ready to go?"

"Yep," Gordon said. "Let's go find Lucy!"

"I like your enthusiasm, kid," Dad said, patting Gordon on the back. Gordon grinned as Mr. Albright handed him a pile of flyers. "Why don't I head south toward Chinatown while you two cover North Beach? We'll meet back here once we've run out of flyers."

"Sounds good," Julie said. "After Gordon and I finish our neighborhood, we'll do Columbus Avenue. It gets plenty of traffic. We can cover both sides of the street." She slipped a roll of masking tape over her wrist and handed Gordon a stapler.

Once they started, Julie thought the system

worked pretty well, even though she and Gordon often found themselves separated. Gordon moved far ahead on his side of the street because all he had to do was bang in two staples, while Julie had to fuss with sticky strips of tape. She was taping a flyer to a kiosk at the entrance to Washington Square Park when she heard Gordon call to her. Looking around, she finally glimpsed him waving his arms and standing at a newspaper booth.

"Albright! We may have a Lucy sighting!"

Julie ran over to the booth. "You have to listen to this guy," Gordon said, nodding at the paper vendor. "You won't believe this!"

"I was telling your friend here," said the newspaper man, "that I saw a parrot this morning over on Telegraph Hill."

Julie looked past the newspaper vendor to Coit Tower, the white column at the top of Telegraph Hill, which was just a few blocks away. "Really?" she said, feeling suddenly upbeat. "That's amazing!"

"I thought I was hallucinating," the vendor said. "I haven't been in the city long, but I never figured it to be parrot country."

"Let's go over there and ask around," Gordon suggested. "Maybe somebody else has seen a parrot there, too."

They thanked the vendor and made their way toward Telegraph Hill. Julie had hiked up to Coit Tower before. The walk was steep and densely lined with trees. Finding a single bird would be tough—and that's if Lucy was still there.

As they started up the first flight of steps, Julie asked a woman coming down if she had seen a parrot anywhere on the hill.

"Sure did," said the woman. "Right up there in the trees by the base of the tower."

This good news gave Julie such a rush of energy that she sprinted ahead, leaving Gordon far behind. "Come on, Gordon," she called after him. "I don't want to miss Lucy!"

Gordon was nearly out of breath when he caught up with her. "How will we catch her?" he panted. "Does she come when you call her name?"

"Good question." Julie thought for a minute. Then she looked her friend in the eyes. "Gordon,

I'll buy you a triple-scoop ice cream cone if you'll do me a huge favor."

Gordon raised his eyebrows. "That bad?"

"I want you to sing the Roto-Rooter jingle with me. If Lucy hears it, she might answer."

Before he could object, Julie started them off. "Call Roto-Rooter, that's the name!" she sang out loudly, but Gordon couldn't go for more than a few words without laughing.

"I can't do this," he finally said, red from laughter—and embarrassment. "What if some-one we know sees us?"

"That doesn't matter," Julie said firmly. "We need to be loud so Lucy will hear us."

"Okay, boss, whatever you say." Gordon wiped the smile off his face and bellowed, "Call Roto-Rooter, that's the name!"

"Better!" said Julie brightly. In spite of the circumstances, now that they were so close to finding Lucy, Julie was having fun. Gordon would sing the first half of the verse, and she would finish the line. Then they would alternate words, or try to sing the song backward.

By the time they reached the top of Telegraph Hill, they were giggling and breathless. Julie called out Lucy's name and heard a fluttering of wings in the leafy branches of a nearby tree.

"Over there!" Gordon shouted. They ran to the tree and peered up into the foliage. "Lucy? Are you in there?"

They ducked as a flock of small green birds flitted out of the tree's canopy into the sky. The flock banked and dove down to land on the seed-scattered ground in front of a bench where an old man was sitting.

"Those birds are parrots!" Gordon exclaimed.

"But not African Greys," Julie said.

"They're canary-winged parakeets," said the man on the bench. He scooped a handful of seeds from a paper bag and tossed them on the ground. "They live up here on Telegraph Hill. A pet owner must have set some birds loose, and now they're breeding in the wild. I come here to feed them occasionally, but they seem to do just fine on their own."

Julie handed him a flyer. "Have you seen

a parrot that looks like this one? She's big and gray, with a bright red tail."

The man shook his head. "I'm afraid not."

"You know what?" Gordon said, turning to Julie. "When the newspaper man told me he saw a parrot, I didn't even ask him what color it was. I never guessed there would be a flock of green ones up here." He shook his head. "Looks like we made this trip for nothing."

But Julie wasn't willing to give up yet. "Just because we saw a bunch of green parrots doesn't mean that the newspaper man didn't see Lucy. Let's go back down and ask him. And maybe by the time we get home, my dad will have heard from the Lings. If it turns out that Lucy's with Uncle Lee, our search will be over." As optimistic as Julie sounded, she could feel herself working hard trying to push her doubts aside.

7
CONFESSIONS

They rushed down the hill, hoping the newspaper vendor would still be there by the time they reached the park. Suddenly, Gordon grabbed Julie's arm. "Julie, hold up!" He pointed to a jogger stretching her legs on a patch of grass nearby. "There's my mom."

"I haven't seen your mom since I moved two years ago. Come on, let's go say hello." She walked up to Gordon's mother, who was wearing a bright pink jogging suit and a terrycloth sweatband on her forehead. "Hi, Mrs. Marino."

"Well, if it isn't Julie Albright," Mrs. Marino said. She stood up and jogged in place. "It is so nice that you and Gordon have reconnected for spring break." She gave Julie a brisk smile. "Will you be playing with Gordon later today?"

Julie squinted. "What do you mean?" She hiked her thumb over her shoulder. "He's right behind m—" But when she turned around, Gordon was nowhere to be seen.

"That's odd," Julie said, spinning around to look for Gordon. "He was here a second ago—he's helping me look for a missing parrot."

Mrs. Marino gave Julie an uncomfortable look. "My son has been acting a bit unusual these days. I'm glad Gordon has a friend he can talk to this week. He won't talk to *me* about what's bugging him."

Julie nodded, feeling awkward. She had noticed that Gordon wasn't his usual self, but he hadn't opened up to *her* either.

Mrs. Marino said good-bye and jogged down the hill. Once she was out of sight, Gordon appeared from behind a nearby tree.

"There you are!" Julie said. "Why did you ditch us?"

Gordon plopped down on a park bench. "Sorry about that, Albright. I just couldn't face my mom right now."

"Why not? Is everything okay, Gordon?"

Gordon looked up at Julie. "No, it's not. My parents are getting a divorce." There were tears in his eyes.

Julie swallowed. *That must be why Gordon has been acting so nervous and gloomy lately,* she realized. "Oh, Gordon. I'm so sorry."

Gordon took a deep breath. "I spend half the week at my mom's house down the street from your dad's, and half the week at my old house, where my dad still lives. My mom and I don't seem to get along well lately. I miss Dad a lot during the week, and my mom just doesn't understand."

Julie sat down next to Gordon. She remembered how deeply her own parents' divorce had affected her and her sister, Tracy, and felt a little pang in her heart. "I know just how you feel."

Gordon quickly wiped his cheek. "I know. If anybody would understand, it's you."

"I guess I was sort of lucky in a way," Julie said. "I had my sister to talk to whenever I was feeling bad." She added, "I know you don't have a brother or sister, but you can still talk to me."

Gordon nodded. "It gets pretty lonely at home. My parents don't pay much attention to me except when they're fighting about me. And whenever it's just me and Mom, she complains about Dad or gets mad at me about the littlest thing." Gordon fumbled with the zipper on his sleeve and let out a sigh. "Listen, can we just focus on finding Lucy? Hanging out with you and the parrot this weekend was helping me forget about everything at home."

Julie nodded. She stood up and pulled Gordon off the bench. "Right. Let's go talk to that newspaper man."

But when they got to the newspaper stand, they were disappointed to find it locked up for the day and the paper seller gone.

"Well, so much for that idea," Julie said. "I guess he sold all his papers."

"Wait—there he is!" Gordon pointed across the park.

Julie shaded her eyes to see the vendor with a sack slung over his shoulder. "Let's go!"

They ran across the grass to catch up with the man.

"Excuse me, sir?" Gordon said, panting heavily.

"Well, if it isn't the young bird-watchers. Did you find that parrot you were looking for?"

"Afraid not," Julie said. "But maybe you can tell us, did the bird you saw look like this one?" She handed the man a flyer. "She's gray with a red tail."

"Kind of. Except the one I saw was green."

Julie's face fell, and her eyes met Gordon's.

"I knew it," Gordon muttered.

"Gee, I'm sorry to disappoint you kids," said the newspaper man. "Say, why don't you give me a stack of those flyers. I'll post one on my stand tomorrow and hand them out to customers."

They thanked the man and started walking home, exhausted and discouraged. When they reached Columbus Avenue, Julie felt a flash of hope. The flyer she had posted at the kiosk was no longer there.

"Gordon, look! I put a flyer on that kiosk, and it's already gone. Maybe somebody found Lucy and took the flyer home to call us!"

Gordon's face brightened. "Let's get to your house. Hurry!" They took off running.

But halfway down the block, Gordon stopped short. "Um, Julie?" He paused, looking up at a light pole where a ripped corner of their flyer hung from a piece of tape. "This one's gone, too."

Julie looked down Columbus Avenue. The flyers had been torn down from the next street-light...and the next...and the next. She looked across the street at the light poles leading back to Washington Square Park. Gordon's flyers had been torn down, too.

"All that hard work!" Gordon wailed. "Who would tear them down?"

"I have no idea." Julie shook her head, stunned. "Maybe someone who doesn't want us to find the bird." She shivered. "Do you think it could be the person who took Lucy?"

Gordon just shrugged and shoved his hands

into his pockets. They walked in silence the rest of the way home.

When they finally reached Julie's house, they found that her dad wasn't home yet. "I don't think he's back from Chinatown," she told Gordon. "While we're waiting for him, let's go to Ivy's house to see if Mr. Shackley is there. Maybe he knows something."

They went across the street, and Julie unlocked the front door. She heard shuffling behind the pocket door and knocked lightly. "Mr. Shackley? It's Julie Albright. The pet sitter?"

Mr. Shackley cracked the door open and didn't say a word. He looked haggard and grumpy, with an unshaven chin and bleary eyes.

Julie swallowed nervously. "Hi, Mr. Shackley. I'm not sure whether you know this, but the Lings' parrot has disappeared, and I was wondering—"

Mr. Shackley opened the door a little wider. "I don't know anything about it. Now what do you want from me?"

Gordon shrank back behind Julie. She cleared her throat. "Did you hear anything strange upstairs in the past twenty-four hours?"

"I didn't hear a thing. In fact, it's been nice and quiet around here without that bird screeching that darn plumbing song all the livelong day."

"I'm sorry, sir," Julie said and looked away. Then she glimpsed one of her flyers lying on the coffee table, a bit crumpled. She felt goose bumps prickle her arms. Could Mr. Shackley have taken down the flyers on Columbus Avenue? "Are you sure there isn't anything else you can tell us?"

Noticing her peering into the living room, the old man slid the door so that only his reddening face was showing. "I don't know what you're suggesting, but I had every right to go up to that bedroom and silence that bird! It was driving me and my wife crazy!"

Julie couldn't believe what she had just heard, but she stayed rooted to the spot, trembling.

"Irv?" called a reedy voice from inside. "Who's out there?"

"Don't worry, Ma," he yelled over his shoulder

to his wife. "It's just that little girl." Suddenly his anger evaporated, and he seemed to shrink inside his oversized robe. Julie half expected him to burst into tears. "Look, I'm sorry about the bird," he said, his voice quivering. "But I can't help you. Now please, leave me and my wife alone." Without another word, he shut the door.

8
Likely Suspects

Julie and Gordon walked back to Julie's house in a daze. "Did you hear that?" Gordon asked. "Mr. Shackley just confessed!"

"I'm not sure," Julie said. She went over Mr. Shackley's words in her head. *I had every right to go up to that bedroom and silence that bird!* "Gordon, do you think he could have done something to Lucy? You don't think he—" She broke off and squeezed her eyes shut. She couldn't bear to think that Lucy might have been hurt—or worse.

"Look, he admitted that he *silenced the bird,*" Gordon said. "I hate to say it, Julie, but that sounds pretty bad."

"It does sound bad," Julie said, "but I don't believe he would hurt her. Maybe he was talking about putting the sheet on the cage yesterday."

"Well, I think it's obvious what happened, but I hope I'm wrong. Anyway, I'd better get home," Gordon said. He lowered his head and started down the street.

Julie went inside and found Dad on the phone in the kitchen. "It's Ivy," he whispered and turned back to his conversation. "Julie just walked in. I'll let you give her the news."

Julie raised her eyebrows. "News?" she said. Her father nodded and handed her the phone.

"Hey, Julie," Ivy said, but her tone was guarded. "Uncle Lee came back in time for the wedding, but Lucy isn't with him. After the ceremony I even asked him if he'd gone to San Francisco to see Lucy, and he said no. He never left Long Beach."

Julie let out a long breath. "Did anyone let him know that Lucy is missing?"

"No way!" Ivy said. "I mean, he's made up with Hannah, and she's told Uncle Lee that he can take Lucy back after the honeymoon. Everyone's so happy! I'd hate to spoil it with bad news."

"I understand. But what if we can't find Lucy before the honeymoon's over?" Julie shut her eyes. *Or ever,* she thought. "Listen, Ivy—Gordon and I looked all over for her today. We put up flyers and even went all the way to the top of Telegraph Hill to search for her." She described their meeting with the newspaper vendor and encounter with the flock of green parakeets, as well as the odd disappearance of the flyers on Columbus Avenue. But she decided to leave out her conversation with Mr. Shackley. After all, she didn't yet have proof that he had done anything to Lucy—and she didn't want to upset Ivy even more by telling her what Gordon thought.

"Sounds like a wild goose chase—or parrot chase! Anyway, you know what I mean," said Ivy. "I know you've been trying hard to find her, and I'm very grateful. But Julie, we *have* to find that parrot!"

Julie could feel Ivy's anxiety from hundreds of miles away. "Ivy, I know we do, but ... " Her voice trailed off into a whisper. "What if—what if we don't?"

"If we don't, well, we'll have to tell him after the honeymoon. I'm afraid that Uncle Lee will take it as a sign of bad luck for their marriage." Ivy sounded shaky, as if she was holding back tears. "I guess I'd better get back to the reception."

Julie ached to say something to reassure her friend, but all she could think of was, "Don't worry, Ivy. I'll ... I'll figure out something."

Julie hung up the phone feeling heavy inside. She looked at the small pile of flyers that she had left. "Should we go make some more copies and repost them?" she asked Dad, who was sitting at the kitchen table.

Dad shook his head. "There's no point in putting up replacements as long as somebody around here is determined to take them down," he replied. "But I covered Chinatown pretty thoroughly, so let's hope those flyers are still up. I even asked the manager at The Happy Panda to translate the flyer into Chinese and put it in the window. Speaking of which—" He took a paper bag off the counter and started pulling out take-out containers. "I picked up some dinner for us. Sesame chicken, your favorite."

Despite her worry, Julie realized how hungry she was as soon as she smelled the sweet sesame sauce. "Thanks, Dad. I'm starving. Is Aunt Maia going to eat with us?"

"She's still at the restaurant. She called to say she'd be home late and said we should eat dinner without her. You'll see her in the morning before she leaves for her first shift."

Julie swallowed her disappointment. She was eager to tell her aunt about everything that had happened. Aunt Maia loved animals and seemed to know a lot about them; maybe she would have some ideas about how to find Lucy.

As they ate their supper, Julie told her father about Mr. Shackley's outburst. "Gordon thinks that Mr. Shackley did something to Lucy. I'm not so sure, but if he hurt one feather on that bird—"

"Now wait a minute—you found the cage and the window both open, right?" asked Dad.

"It's possible that Mr. Shackley let the bird fly out the window, but let's not jump to conclusions."

Julie nodded. "I'll visit Mr. Shackley again tomorrow. Maybe with a good night's sleep, he will be willing to explain what he meant." She yawned and started packing up the leftovers.

"You look tired, honey. I'll take care of the cleanup, and you go get some rest." Dad took the carton from her hand and kissed the top of her head.

Julie went upstairs and changed into her pajamas. She lay down on her bed and closed her eyes, but her mind was racing.

Could Lucy's chatter have been so unbearable that Mr. Shackley had released her? Wouldn't he have realized that a pet, especially an exotic one, might not be able to survive on its own? Mr. Shackley might be grumpy, but he didn't seem cruel. And what about the Lings, who were generously letting him and his wife stay in their house? Lucy belonged to them. Would he really have done such an awful thing to the people who were being so kind to him and his wife?

Julie tried to picture where Lucy could be right now if Mr. Shackley had released her from her cage. Had she joined the flock of small green parrots on Telegraph Hill? Was she flying over Chinatown? Was she looking for Uncle Lee? Julie wondered if Lucy was happy to be flying free, as Aunt Maia had suggested.

Giving up on sleep, Julie reached down and lifted Nutmeg onto the bed. "I don't know what I'd do if you went missing," she said, rubbing her nose on Nutmeg's silky head. Julie set the bunny on the floor and watched her hop around the room as she thought over the day's events. It was obvious that Mr. Shackley was the most likely suspect, given what he had said to them that afternoon. Besides, Mr. Shackley had the easiest access to Andrew's room—all he had to do was slide open the pocket door and go right up the stairs.

And yet, unlike Gordon, Julie wasn't quite ready to believe that Mr. Shackley would be so unkind to the Lings—or the bird—as to release Lucy out the window.

Suddenly Julie had an awful thought. Gordon

had been so confident that Mr. Shackley was guilty. Why was he so quick to pin the blame on the old man?

Julie frowned, recalling the last time they visited Lucy together. Gordon had said that he could use the company of a bird like Lucy.

Could *Gordon* have taken Lucy?

Julie thought back to earlier in the day. Why would Gordon help look for the parrot if he knew where she was all along? Well, maybe he had helped post flyers to keep her from suspecting him.

But how would he have gotten Lucy out of the Lings' house in the first place?

Julie sucked in her breath. *Of course!* Gordon had gone back upstairs to fetch his jacket after they had said good-bye to Lucy. He could have hidden her under the jacket and taken her home with him.

Then Julie remembered what Gordon had said about his mom's strict no-pet policy. If Gordon had brought the bird back to his house, would he really have been able to hide her squawking from his mother?

Besides, Julie had just seen Gordon's mom at the park. If Mrs. Marino knew about her son's new pet, wouldn't she have said something when Julie told her about the missing bird?

No, Julie decided, it didn't seem possible that Gordon had been keeping Lucy at his house this whole time.

"I'd better get some sleep," she told Nutmeg. "Otherwise I might start suspecting *myself*!"

9
A Terrible Discovery

The next morning, Julie and Dad had already finished breakfast and were washing the dishes when Maia finally came downstairs, looking flustered.

"Morning, sis," Dad said to Maia. "I saved you some skillet potatoes. Would you like some toast?"

"I have to be at work in twenty minutes, so I'll take my breakfast to go," said Maia, pulling a banana off the bunch. She stepped up to the sink and tugged gently on Julie's braid. "Hey, you. Can I talk to you for a second before I leave?"

Julie followed her aunt into the living room and dropped down next to her on the couch. "Your dad told me everything when I got home last night. I just wanted to say how sorry I am about Lucy. I know this must be very upsetting for you," Maia continued. "I wish I could stick around to help you today. But while I'm gone, try calling this number." She handed Julie a strip of paper.

Julie studied the phone number scrawled across the paper. "What is this?"

"The Animal Switchboard. They're volunteers who assist people who have lost an animal, or found one, or just need some help with their pets. Maybe they'll have some ideas on how to get Lucy back."

"Thanks," Julie said, hugging her aunt. "And good luck at work today."

"Thanks, sweetie," Maia said. She gave Julie a squeeze and started out the door, grabbing her silk scarf and keys from the bowl in the foyer before shutting the door behind her.

Julie suddenly flushed with an uneasy sense of déjà vu. The macramé key chain. The silk scarf. Julie closed her eyes and thought back to yesterday morning, in the moments as she was leaving the house right before she had found

Lucy's cage empty. She had gone to the foyer and felt around in the bowl but couldn't find the macramé key chain. Then Dad had found it on the table under Maia's scarf.

With a sinking heart, Julie recalled the conversation they'd had at the dinner table the night before Julie had discovered that Lucy was missing. Maia had suggested that Julie let Lucy out of her cage and had seemed upset when Julie told her she didn't want to go against Uncle Lee's directions. In fact, Maia had excused herself from the table right then, grabbed a key from the bowl, and gone out to get some fresh air. Could Maia have taken the macramé key chain from the bowl and used it to get into the Lings' house? Julie tried to block out the image of Maia entering Andrew's room, opening the window and Lucy's cage, and setting the bird free.

"Oh, Aunt Maia," Julie whispered, dropping her face into her hands. *Maia is so eager to help now,* Julie thought. *Does she feel guilty about Lucy?*

She glanced at the phone number on the piece of paper Maia had handed her. "Might as

well give it a try," she murmured and headed
to the kitchen. When the Animal Switchboard
volunteer answered, Julie introduced herself
and quickly told the woman about Lucy's
disappearance.

"I'm sorry," said the volunteer. "We haven't
had a report of an African Grey."

Julie bit her lip. "The Humane Society didn't
have any news either. We put up flyers yesterday but haven't heard a word," Julie said.
"This was my last hope. What do you think the
chances are of finding her?"

"Well, as you probably already know," the
volunteer said, "African Greys don't take well
to new environments and strangers—especially
when they have been with the same owner for a
long time."

"Lucy was very attached to her first owner,"
Julie said. She thought of Uncle Lee and Lucy
on the day she had met them. They were such a
happy pair—and now it seemed likely that Julie
would soon be breaking Uncle Lee's heart with
the bad news.

"I'm sorry," said the volunteer. She hesitated and then added, "I hate to tell you this, Julie, but African Greys are quite valuable because of their intelligence and speaking ability. Does Lucy talk?"

"Yes," Julie said. "And sings, too."

She heard a sigh on the other end. "She sounds like a wonderful bird. Unfortunately, somebody who finds her could easily sell her for a lot of money."

Julie flinched at the idea of someone selling sweet Lucy for some quick cash. "That's terrible!"

"Have you ruled out the possibility that she was stolen?" the volunteer asked. "We haven't had any reports of stolen parrots for a while, but when it does happen, it's usually because somebody wants to make some easy money."

"Whoever took Lucy didn't take her cage. Maybe the thief had a smaller cage of his own that was easier to sneak around with," Julie speculated. Then she recalled what Uncle Lee had said about Lucy needing time to adjust to a new caretaker. "But would Lucy let a stranger just take her?"

The volunteer confirmed that parrots could be unwilling captives in unfamiliar hands. "They will fight when they feel threatened and are excellent escape artists. Do you know if Lucy's wings were trimmed?" she asked. "If so, she wouldn't be able to fly away."

Julie didn't think they were. "But if African Greys are good at escapes, maybe she'll find her way home."

But, Julie wondered, would Lucy regard Ivy's house as home? Or would she try to make her way to Long Beach, where she had lived with Uncle Lee? Julie thought of one of her favorite books, *The Incredible Journey,* about two dogs and a cat who travel across hundreds of miles of wilderness to return to their owners. Certainly, she knew, some birds could migrate hundreds, even thousands, of miles. Could Lucy make it all the way from San Francisco to Long Beach, in southern California?

"It doesn't hurt to hope," said the volunteer, breaking into Julie's thoughts.

Julie thanked the volunteer and left her

address and phone number in case the Switch-board received any reports about Lucy. She hung up and leaned her back against the wall. *Stolen and sold?* she thought. *But who would take her?* Ivy's family had only just gotten Lucy—how would a thief even know there was a valuable parrot living at the Lings' house?

Dejected, Julie wandered to the living room and stared up at Ivy's window. By now she had hoped to have at least one lead, *something* encour-aging to share with Ivy. She tried to drum up some optimism. If Lucy was already in the hands of a new owner, that person might possibly see the flyers that hadn't been ripped down and do the right thing by calling her. On the other hand, if Mr. Shackley or Maia had let Lucy go free, she could be anywhere, and Julie might never find her. And if Lucy had been stolen—well, a professional bird thief would probably take her to another city to sell, to avoid attracting the attention of local authorities who might have heard reports of a missing African Grey.

Suddenly, Julie saw something gray moving

in Ivy's window. Had Lucy been hiding inside the Lings' house after all? She looked closer and found that it was only Jasmine, the gray cat, on Ivy's windowsill, rubbing against the glass. *She must be hungry,* Julie realized. The cats needed feeding. She sighed. Although she didn't want to, she knew she had to talk to Mr. Shackley one more time—for Lucy's sake.

She let Dad know she'd be back soon and stepped outside. As she closed the door behind her, something unfamiliar caught her eye—a pile of dark fabric bunched into a corner of the concrete stoop, where the railing met the wall of the house. Julie picked up the pile and shook it out. It wasn't fabric—it was heavy leather. She recognized the flashy zippers on the sleeves. *Gordon's jacket.*

She was sure that he had been wearing the jacket when he left her house to go home yesterday. Had he taken it off as he was leaving? Or had he come back and left it here on purpose?

I should get it back to him before his mom thinks he's lost another jacket, Julie thought. After she fed the cats, she would take it to his mom's house down the street. If Gordon was there, she decided, she would come right out and ask him once and for all whether he had taken Lucy. *But first things first,* she told herself. She dusted off the jacket and marched across the street to the Lings' house.

Inside the front hall, she knocked on the pocket door and felt both disappointment and relief when no one answered. Once upstairs, she gave the cats some petting and tummy rubs, smiling at their grateful purring. She rinsed their bowls in the bathroom sink and set out some fresh food and water.

As the cats ate, she went into Andrew's room. The eerie quiet overwhelmed her. In Lucy's absence, the room felt darker, even with the bright shaft of sunlight from the window piercing the gloom. She went over to Lucy's cage. The gate still hung open, and the crumpled white sheet and safety clip were where she had left them on the desk the day before.

Julie picked up the clip and inspected it. It was scarred with nicks as though somebody had tried to pry it off the cage with something sharp. She wondered why she hadn't noticed that before. Had the thief used a knife? *That's odd,* she thought. *All he had to do was snap the clip open with his fingers.*

With Gordon's jacket slung over her arm, Julie left the Lings' house more miserable than ever. She had another dreadful task ahead of her—confronting Gordon and asking him whether he had taken Lucy. She walked down the block until she came to the green house with white trim and rang the doorbell.

"Why, Julie!" said Mrs. Marino, opening the front door. "What a surprise. I thought Gordon was meeting you at your father's house."

"Meeting me? At my father's house?" Julie repeated.

"That son of mine. So forgetful!" She rolled her eyes. "He said that he had forgotten something at your house and he was going to pick it up from you. I'm surprised you didn't pass him on your way over."

"We must have just missed each other. I was

across the street feeding the Lings' cats."

"Well, I'll tell him you stopped by." Mrs. Marino started to close the door.

"Actually, Mrs. Marino? I came to return Gordon's jacket." She hesitated. "That must be what he forgot at my house."

"That?" Mrs. Marino said, with a poke at the leather bundle in Julie's arms. "That's not Gordon's."

Julie wasn't sure what to say. She didn't want to argue with Mrs. Marino. "Um, well ... he was wearing it yesterday. I'm pretty sure it's his."

Mrs. Marino took the jacket from Julie's hands and inspected it. "I assure you that this couldn't belong to my son. Do you see this label?" She showed Julie the inside of the collar. "This jacket is from the Lombard Leather Boutique. Gordon has been saving up for a new jacket, but he'd never be able to afford one of this quality, even if I tripled his allowance."

Julie had to agree. She and Ivy had wandered into Lombard Leather last summer, glanced at one steep price tag, and immediately backed out of the shop. When Gordon had shown her the jacket yesterday, she had wondered how he could suddenly afford it, but now she realized that it was impossible.

Julie took back the jacket, feeling awkward and confused. "I guess I was wrong. Sorry to bother you, Mrs. Marino."

"It's quite all right, Julie. And I do hope you find the owner of that fine jacket."

Julie said good-bye and turned to go home. She tried to concentrate on Lucy, but her confusing conversation with Mrs. Marino had set her head spinning. There was no question that this *was* Gordon's jacket, she knew. But if he couldn't afford the jacket on his own, and his mother hadn't purchased it for him, where had he gotten the money to buy it?

10
THE FIRE-ESCAPE FEAT

Julie stopped short in the middle of the sidewalk, unable to breathe. A horrible new theory took shape in her head: Gordon had stolen Lucy—but not to keep her as a pet. Instead, he had sold her and used the money to buy the leather jacket.

She continued down the sidewalk toward home, dizzy with questions. This business with the jacket made Gordon's motive clear. And now she realized that she had been right that he hadn't carried Lucy home with him under his jacket—once he found a buyer to take Lucy, he must have returned to Ivy's house to steal the parrot. But how could he have gotten past the locked front door at the Lings'?

Instead of going home, Julie crossed the

street and returned to Ivy's house. Was there another entrance? Then she remembered—the fire escape led straight up to Andrew's window at the back of the house. Gordon himself had pointed it out! But she was certain she had closed and locked Andrew's window before they'd left that day. So how could Gordon have gotten in?

Stepping into the alley behind Ivy's house, Julie gazed up at the fire escape. There were two ladders: one leading down from a platform on the third floor, where Andrew's room was, to the second floor, and one that could go from the second floor to the ground. But the fire escape was built for people to climb down—not up. The ladder to the ground was partly retracted, and Julie knew that the Lings would have to push an iron lever on the second-floor platform to let the stairs down if they ever needed to use the fire escape to get to the street. Dad's house had a similar fire escape in the back.

So how would Gordon reach the bottom ladder from the street? There wasn't anything in the alley to stack and climb up, just a metal Dumpster with nothing inside it except a broken terra-cotta pot and a headless broomstick. She looked at the Lings' kitchen window and eyed the distance between the edge of the sill and the bottom rung of the ladder. Maybe Gordon could have run hard at the window and caught a toe on the sill, using it as leverage to jump up and catch the ladder. It wouldn't be easy, but if Gordon could do standing backflips on the Sierra Vista playground, he could probably accomplish this gymnastic feat.

Julie was a basketball player and a pretty good jumper herself, so she decided to try and see if she could reach the ladder the way Gordon might have. She gently laid Gordon's jacket on the pavement and stepped back a few paces. With a running start, she leaped onto the narrow sill and bounced, stretching her arms and grasping for the ladder. "Almost!" she gasped, and tried again.

"What is all this noise?" said a gravelly voice behind her. She spun around and found

Mr. Shackley standing with his hands on his hips. He looked more bright-eyed than she had ever seen him before.

"Mr. Shackley! I'm sorry, I didn't think you were home. I knocked on your door a little while ago and no one answered."

"My wife had another checkup this morning, and we just got back. When I stepped into the house, I heard all your ruckus at the window and assumed we were being robbed! Now, what on earth are you doing? Did you lose your key to the front door?"

"I—well, you see, I'm investigating what might have happened to the parrot and—" Remembering suddenly that Gordon wasn't her only suspect, Julie stopped abruptly. Then she stood taller and looked the old man straight in the eye. "Mr. Shackley, did you release Lucy from her cage?"

Mr. Shackley looked stumped and didn't say a word.

"I . . . I just thought—based on what you said yesterday—about *silencing* the bird?"

Mr. Shackley lifted his hand to his forehead. "I merely meant that I had covered the cage on Saturday afternoon to quiet the parrot. The bird had been squawking away since your morning visit, and my wife needed to rest. I had intended to remove the sheet after our nap, but I simply forgot. I didn't mean to frighten you."

"That makes sense, I guess," Julie mumbled.

Then Mr. Shackley bowed his head, and she could see that he was ashamed. "I'm afraid that I was quite rude to you and your friend yesterday," he said. "I am sorry about that. My wife gave me a good scolding after you left. I have not been sleeping well lately, and it has turned me into a bit of a grouch. As soon as I fall asleep, I wake up in a panic that my wife has gotten sick again." He continued, "Mrs. Shackley and I feel just awful that the parrot has disappeared. We didn't realize that she had gone missing until we saw your flyer posted down the street. But when we saw that lady pulling down all of your flyers, we figured that the bird had been found."

What lady? Julie wondered. *Surely he couldn't mean Aunt Maia—could he?* "Can you tell me what the lady looked like?" Julie asked. "The one who was pulling down the flyers?"

"Let's see. Ah, yes, I believe she was wearing a pink tracksuit. She looked as if she must have been out for a run because she was wearing a sweatband on her head."

Julie paused. Mrs. Marino had been wearing a pink jogging suit and sweatband that day on Telegraph Hill. But why would Gordon's mother take down all the flyers?

Maybe she's trying to protect her son from getting caught, Julie thought. She examined the fire escape again.

Mr. Shackley followed her gaze. "So, what does all of this have to do with the fire escape?"

"I'm, uh, testing a theory," Julie told him. "Do you remember the boy who was with me when I came by last night? I'm wondering if he was able to climb up to that top window and break in."

Mr. Shackley scratched his chin. "Well,

I assure you he couldn't have gotten through the front door. Mrs. Shackley makes me double-check the lock every time we enter and leave the house. So I suppose that does leave the fire escape." He craned his neck to look at the ladder on the second floor. "I don't want you to get hurt trying to get up there. How about I give you a hand?"

"You wouldn't mind?" Julie asked.

"It's the least I can do." He eyed the kitchen window, the Dumpster, and the ladder. "Now, let's think about this a little harder. Could this fellow have used the window ledge as a stair step to reach the lip of the garbage bin?"

"I bet he could have," Julie said. "I'll try it." She pulled herself up onto the window ledge. Mr. Shackley took her hand and spotted her as she stepped onto the edge of the Dumpster. She held on to the top of the window frame to steady herself and then reached up with her other hand to try to grab the bottom rung of the ladder, but her fingers didn't even graze it. "No luck," she grunted.

"Try this," Mr. Shackley said, pulling the broomstick from the Dumpster and handing it to her. "Do you see that lever up there next to the ladder? See if you can reach it with the broomstick." Julie reached up and tried to keep the end of the stick steady as she poked at the lever. Sure enough, after a couple of attempts the ladder slid down to the ground. "We did it!" she cried, but her sense of triumph was short-lived, quickly replaced by the heart-sinking realization that if *she* could do it with only a bit of help, Gordon could probably have managed it on his own.

Julie carefully lowered herself and jumped to the ground.

"Now, shall we go up and test that window?" asked Mr. Shackley.

Julie gave him a surprised look. "Do you think you can make it up the ladder?"

Mr. Shackley laughed. "I think I still have plenty of pep left, but maybe for safety's sake we should go up using the stairs *inside* the house." Mr. Shackley shoved the ladder upward, and the lever clicked, locking the ladder in place. Julie picked up the leather jacket and followed him around the house and up the front steps.

Once they were upstairs in Andrew's room, Julie pressed lightly on the window latch with her thumb to pop it open.

Mr. Shackley stuck his head through the opening. "I may still have some pep, but I'm not as limber as I used to be. Think you can climb over the sill?"

"Sure can," said Julie. Mr. Shackley helped her as she hoisted one leg and then the other through the window and jumped onto the platform outside. "Why don't you lock me out, and I'll see if I can jimmy it open from the outside?"

Mr. Shackley shut the window firmly and fastened the latch. "Ready!" he called through the glass.

Julie inspected the window. There were no signs that someone had tried to pry it open. She ran her fingers around the edge of the frame. There was very little to grab to slide it open, so she tried pushing the frame sideways.

It wouldn't budge. She attempted everything she could think of, even giving the window frame a few smacks for good measure. "It's shut tight!" she called to Mr. Shackley through the closed window.

Julie didn't want to admit it, but she was out of ideas.

Mr. Shackley popped the window open again and helped her back inside. As they walked back downstairs, he said, "I don't think the boy could have gotten in using the fire escape unless the window was already open when you left the house."

"But I'm certain I closed the window, Mr. Shackley. I was so careful. It was the last thing I did before we left the room. And Gordon came out with me—" She paused and drew in a quick breath. "But then Gordon said that he had forgotten his jacket and went back into the room to get it." She paused, working out his scheme in her head before continuing. "Maybe he made his plan while he was up there! After all, he knew he couldn't take the parrot right then because his mom would notice if he brought it home. So he popped the window open so that he could get back in later to take Lucy and sell her."

Mr. Shackley nodded. "That's certainly possible—" he started but was distracted by his wife sliding open the pocket door.

"Irv, honey," she said. "I could use your help organizing my pills."

"I'll be right in, Ma," he said. "Julie, this is my wife. Gloria, this is Julie, the Lings' pet sitter."

"Nice to meet you, Mrs. Shackley," Julie said. "I'm glad to hear you're feeling better."

Mrs. Shackley gave Julie a smile. "Thank you, Julie. And I do hope you have some luck finding that poor bird."

"Thanks for your help, Mr. Shackley," Julie said as she shifted Gordon's jacket to her other arm and stuck out her free hand for a handshake.

Mr. Shackley chuckled and took Julie's hand. "You're a smart girl, Julie. I'm sure you'll figure things out before long, but I'll let you know if I come up with any more information. Until then, I wish you the best of luck."

11
Getting Some Answers

Julie ran back home and burst into the kitchen, eager to tell her dad all about her encounter with Mr. Shackley.

"Hiya, kiddo," Dad greeted her. "Gordon left a few minutes ago. He said he had forgotten his jacket on our porch. We didn't find it out there, so I figured you must have it. We waited around for you to come back, but after a while he had to go home. What have you been up to?"

"Boy, do I have a lot to tell you," Julie said. But just as she was about to start, they heard the front door open. "Is that you, Gordon?" Julie called.

But it wasn't Gordon who appeared in the kitchen doorway—it was Maia. She looked at them with red, wet eyes. Julie bit her lip. *Was Maia about to confess that she had set Lucy free?*

Julie forced herself to speak. "Are you okay, Aunt Maia? Aren't you supposed to be at the restaurant?"

"I don't belong there," Maia whimpered. "My boss thinks I'd make a better server than a cook. He told me to come back if I want to wait tables. Otherwise, I'm out of a job." She went on to tell them about her lunch shift. She had struggled to keep up with orders and was so flustered that she couldn't remember the recipes that the chef had taught her. "And so I improvised," she said. "But a lot of the customers sent the food I cooked back to the kitchen." She grabbed a tissue and blew her nose. "I have no trouble cooking alone in a kitchen with dishes I'm familiar with, but I guess I'm just no good at working with someone else's recipes."

Julie and Dad shared a look. Julie had no doubt that he, too, was thinking about the fishy greens and too-spicy tofu Maia had served over the weekend. Dad gave Julie a small smile and winked to signal her to be polite.

"Gosh, I'm sorry, Aunt Maia," Julie said.

"I thought the food you prepared for us was delicious." She caught herself, not wanting to lie. "Well, most of it was."

"That's kind of you, Julie," Maia said. "You know, I've always dreamed of opening my own vegetarian restaurant someday. I guess those plans are out the window."

"Don't give up, Mary," Dad said. "Maybe this is a blessing in disguise. Owning a restaurant requires an understanding of making the food *and* serving it. Maybe you'll learn more than you expect from waiting tables."

Maia thought about that. "You might have a point. And I can always keep on practicing my own recipes at home."

"And we'll be your loyal taste testers," Julie said, nudging her dad.

Dad nodded. "Count me in!"

Maia gave a sad smile and squeezed Julie's hand. "You both have been very supportive over the past few days, and here I've been focusing on my own problems when you have so much to worry about with Lucy missing. That poor bird, lost and alone in the big city."

Julie raised her eyebrows. "But Aunt Maia, I thought you were against keeping pets in cages."

"Well, I'm sure that parrots are happiest with their flocks in the wild," Maia said. "But for a bird that has been hand-raised, like Lucy, its owner becomes a substitute for the flock. And the bird can't necessarily survive on its own."

Julie couldn't help blurting out what she was thinking. "So you didn't release Lucy from her cage?"

"Me? Goodness no! Why would I do a thing like that?"

Julie felt embarrassed. "Well, you *did* tell me that Nutmeg would be happier with more room to move around. And the other night you said that you would be depressed if you were cooped up like Lucy, and then you left the house upset. The next morning, right before I discovered that Lucy had disappeared, I couldn't find the Lings' key chain. When I found it under your scarf, I didn't know what to think! To be honest, I've been suspecting everyone lately."

Maia put her hand to her cheek. "Oh, Julie, I was so frazzled yesterday as I was leaving for the chef training," she said, blowing a stray curl from her eyes. "I couldn't find my house keys in my purse, where I thought I'd put them. So I stirred around in the bowl in the foyer, and there they were. I must have accidentally swept your key chain out of the bowl. Then I decided that it was too warm out for a scarf, so I tossed it on the table."

"Well, that explains it," Dad said. "Why don't you tell us about your other suspects, Julie."

Julie described her suspicions about Mr. Shackley and their encounter in the alley that afternoon. Then she told them everything she had discovered about Gordon, as well as Mr. Shackley's description of the woman in a pink jogging suit taking down the flyers on Columbus Avenue. She showed them the leather jacket and repeated what Mrs. Marino had said about the label and Gordon's allowance. "I also talked to the lady at the Animal Switchboard,"

Julie continued. "She told me that African Greys are so valuable that thieves steal them and resell them for a lot of money. So I started to wonder about Gordon and his jacket. After all, other than you two and Mr. Shackley, Gordon was the only person who knew about Lucy and knew that the Lings were out of town."

Mr. Albright leaned back in his chair. "Gordon did seem nervous when he was here this morning, and he seemed very determined to get his jacket back. Still, it's a pretty awful thing to do to you, to Ivy—and to the parrot. What do you think would drive him to do something like that?"

Julie hesitated. "Things have been difficult for him at home. His parents are going through a divorce, and he's—he's not getting much attention from them."

Dad nodded and put his arm around Julie's shoulder. "We know how hard it can be for a family going through a divorce."

Maia looked pensive. "If Gordon did steal Lucy to sell her, he wouldn't get very far with her without a cage. He probably took her to one of the local pet shops to try to sell her."

"Perhaps you should call Gordon and clear things up with him," Dad suggested. "If he confesses, I'm sure he can tell you where he sold her."

"Good idea," Julie said, jumping out of her seat. She gripped the phone tightly and asked for Gordon when his mother answered.

Mrs. Marino clucked her tongue. "Once again, dear, you missed him by a couple of minutes. He just left to have dinner with his father."

"Oh, okay," Julie said. But she couldn't hang up without some answers. "Um, Mrs. Marino? Remember when we were searching for that parrot? Well, I was wondering—"

"Oh, about that," Mrs. Marino interrupted her. "When I saw you this morning I forgot to tell you about the flyers."

Julie gulped. She hadn't expected Mrs. Marino to confess her involvement in Gordon's scheme without some prodding. "What about the flyers?" she asked.

"I'm sorry to tell you this, Julie, but the

North Beach Neighborhood Committee forbids the posting of flyers on our streets. As the president of the committee, I was obligated to remove them on our street and on Columbus Avenue."

"Oh," said Julie. "I . . . I didn't know."

"Until I spoke to you on Telegraph Hill, I didn't realize that the flyers were yours," Mrs. Marino added. "And I felt terrible that I had torn them down—even if all I had done was carry out my civic duty—so I decided to help you. On my way home, I retrieved the flyers from the bin where I'd discarded them at the community recycling center and hand-delivered them to all the homes in the neighborhood."

"Wow, that was nice of you," Julie said. "Thank you." It was obvious to her now that Mrs. Marino knew nothing about Gordon selling Lucy to get money for the leather jacket. Julie didn't want him to get into trouble, so she decided against accusing him of stealing and selling Lucy outright. But she couldn't see any reason not to tell Mrs. Marino about the jacket.

She drew in a shaky breath.

"Mrs. Marino, I know you said today that the leather jacket I brought over wasn't Gordon's. But I am positive that I saw him wearing that jacket yesterday. He showed it off to me very proudly and said he had just gotten it. Plus, my dad said that Gordon stopped by to pick up the jacket this afternoon."

There was silence on the other end of the line. Finally Mrs. Marino said, "I see."

Julie pressed on. "So my question is: do you have any idea where he might have found the money to buy the jacket?"

This time, Gordon's mother was silent for so long that Julie wasn't sure they were still connected. "Hello?" she asked. "Are you there?"

"Uh, yes. I heard you." Mrs. Marino's voice had changed from bright and musical to cautious and brooding. "Now that I think of it, I am quite sure I know how Gordon got the money for that jacket." Then the line went dead.

12
A Parrot's Song

Julie slept fitfully that night and dreamed
of Lucy, miserable and lonely, locked in a cage
in her new owner's basement. She woke up
feeling groggy, as if her head had been stuffed
with cotton. She fed Nutmeg and got dressed.
As the rabbit bounced happily around the room,
Julie thought about the past few days. Lucy was
out there somewhere, probably wishing she
were home.

Julie gave Nutmeg a final pat and went
downstairs to the kitchen. Maia and Dad were
at the table sipping coffee.

"Good morning," Julie grumbled and sank
into her chair. She turned to Dad. "Do you think
I should call Gordon?"

"First have some breakfast," said Maia. She

set a bowl of oatmeal in front of Julie, who wrinkled her nose at the bland-looking oats. "Here, try this," Maia said. She stirred in some brown sugar and sliced a banana over the bowl. "Just to show you that I'm not so bad at improvising."

Julie gave a small smile and dug in. Once she had scraped the last bits from the bowl, she looked at Dad. "Can we try calling now?"

He checked his watch. "It's probably an okay time to call."

Julie went to the wall phone and dialed Gordon's number. Ater several rings, she shook her head. "No answer," she said, and hung up. "Well, I can't just sit here doing nothing. A pet store could be selling Lucy to a new owner right now, and then we'd never find her."

Maia turned to Dad. "I have an idea. I'll go with Julie to the local pet stores to see if we can find any leads. Dan, you stay here in case Gordon calls."

"Thanks, Aunt Maia," Julie said, relieved to be doing something useful. She pulled out the phone book, opened the yellow pages to the "P" section, and drew her finger down the page. "Let's see here: package delivery, paper products, party supplies…ah, here we are—pet stores." Maia brought over a piece of paper, and Julie wrote down the three stores within walking distance. "Let's get going!"

"Good luck, you two," Dad said.

"We could start at Emily's Animal Emporium," Maia suggested, looking at Julie's list as they headed out the door.

"That's where I got Nutmeg," Julie said. "It's just two blocks away."

They reached the store in no time. Julie hurried through the aisles, looking for the bird section. But all she found were exotic fish swimming in aquariums, hamsters spinning on their wheels, and a litter of puppies playing in a window display.

Then she heard a familiar noise—a fire-truck siren. It grew louder and louder. "Lucy?" Julie called across the store. "Where are you?" When a real fire truck sped past the store windows, its red lights flashing and sirens blaring, she

realized her mistake. Still, she wasn't ready
to give up, so she marched over to the young
employee filing her nails behind the cash regis-
ter. "Excuse me, do you sell any parrots?"

The teenage cashier snapped her bubble gum.
"No birds . . . except for this one." She reached
behind her to a wall of dog toys, pulled a stuffed
toucan off the rack, and squeezed its belly to make
it squeak. "Will this do?"

"Um, no," Julie said. "I'm looking for a live
one. Thanks anyway." She pushed out of the
store with Maia close behind.

"Hey, Miss Speedy, slow down. The next
closest pet store is thataway," Maia said, pointing in the opposite direction.

Julie pivoted and headed up the street, with
Maia at her side. "We're going to find Lucy at
the next store," Julie said. "I can feel it!"

But when they arrived at Discount Pets, they
found a vacant store with two signs on the door.
One said, "Going Out of Business." The other
read, "Sorry, We're Closed."

Julie huffed. "What do we have to do, visit

every store in San Francisco?"

Maia squeezed Julie's shoulder. "I don't think it will come to that. We still have one more store on our list. And if we don't find her there, maybe by the time we get home, your dad will have some news from Gordon or his mom."

Julie checked the list. "Feathered Friends. With 'feathered' in the store's name, they'll sell birds for sure! Come on, it's this way." She grabbed Maia's hand and pulled her along.

When they reached the shop, Julie burst through the door and followed the tweets and chirps to the back of the store. There she found a mustachioed man scooping piles of seed from a bucket into the birdcages.

"Hello," he said, looking up. "Can I help you?"

"I sure hope so. I'm looking for an African Grey parrot," Julie said, crossing her fingers.

"Hmm, sorry. We don't sell tropical birds here—just your standard finches and canaries."

Julie's throat tightened with disappointment. "Oh, okay," she said. "Thanks anyway."

"But there's a shop that sells parrots just

down the street."

"There is?" Maia asked. "It wasn't listed in the phone book."

"They only opened a month ago. It's just two blocks down on Pacific Avenue. You can't miss it."

"Thanks, mister!" Julie said. She and Maia dashed out the door and ran down the street to Pacific Avenue. On the corner, Pirate Pete's Parrot Palace was hard to miss. The storefront was decorated with colorful painted feathers. Above the entrance hung a sign featuring an eye-patched, peg-legged pirate with a parrot on his shoulder.

A little bell jingled as Julie pushed through the door. She was immediately overwhelmed by the familiar sounds of parrot squawks and screeches. It wasn't a big store, but there were cages everywhere, each holding a colorful bird.

"Ahoy, matey!" a gruff voice called from somewhere in the back of the store. "Take a look around. I'll be with you in a moment."

"Hello!" said a brilliantly colored macaw as Julie approached its cage.

"Hello to you," Julie replied, gasping at the thousand-dollar price tag on the parrot's cage.

Julie walked from cage to cage, peering at each parrot as if it might have an answer for her. There were blue and green and yellow parakeets, green and red lovebirds, rainbow-feathered sun conures, pale pink cockatoos, and gray cockatiels with orange cheeks—but no African Greys.

Hopes flagging, she sang out, "Call Roto-Rooter, that's the name ... "

"And away go troubles down the drain!"

Julie spun around and looked at Maia with wide eyes. Maia put her hands up. "It wasn't me, I promise," she said.

Julie tried again, a bit louder, "Call Roto-Rooter! That's the name!"

"And away go troubles down the drain!" came the reply.

Was it possible that one of these birds knew Lucy's favorite song, too? As she reached the end of the row of cages, she decided to try another trick. "Lucy, say hello to Julie."

"Hey, Alley-oop!"

Julie's heart leaped. The squawk was unmistakable—it had to be her. But where was it coming from?

Between two large cages, Julie spotted a doorway. She pushed through the swinging door into a storage room. There was Lucy, beautiful Lucy, bobbing her head and dancing across the perch in a small cage.

"Lucy!" Julie cried. "Aunt Maia, she's in here!"

As Julie reached up to touch the padlock that hung from the cage door, she heard quick, heavy footsteps approaching the storeroom and whirled around. The shopkeeper planted himself before her.

"What are you doing in here?" he bellowed. "This room is private!"

"Th—this bird . . . she—" Julie stammered.

He stepped between Julie and the small cage. "This bird's not for sale."

13
BANANAS

"You don't understand," Julie said. "I *know* that parrot."

The man stood with his arms crossed. "Can you prove it?"

Maia peered over the shopkeeper's shoulder and gave Julie a reassuring nod.

"Yes, sir," she replied. "My name's Julie, and this is my Aunt Maia. The parrot's name is Lucy."

"Awk!" squawked Lucy.

Julie stuck out her hand. "Nice to meet you, mister—?"

"The name's Pete," he said, his mood softening. "Pirate Pete."

"Well, Pirate Pete, I can tell you a few of the tricks I've seen her do," Julie went on, standing a little taller. "She sings the Roto-Rooter song and crows like a rooster. Plus, she does a perfect imitation of a fire-truck siren. Oh, and she loves bananas."

The man rubbed his chin. "Bananas, you say?"

The bell on the door jingled, signaling the arrival of a new customer.

"I'll be back in a moment," Pete said to Julie and Maia.

They heard him greet the new customer using his pirate accent. "Ahoy, matey! How can I help ye?"

Then Julie heard a familiar voice: "We're looking for an African Grey parrot. Her name's Lucy."

Julie couldn't believe her ears. "That's Gordon!" she whispered to Maia.

They hurried to the front of the store, where they were surprised to find not just Gordon but also Mr. Albright and Mrs. Marino.

"Julie!" Gordon cried. "Lucy's here!"

"I know," Julie said, eyeing him warily.

"How could you do this, Gordon?"

Gordon looked stunned. "I . . . I didn't—wait, what do you mean?"

Julie frowned. "You sold her to Pirate Pete to get money for the leather jacket, right?" At his incredulous look, she felt her anger rising. "Come on, Gordon, how else would you know she was here?" Looking desperate, Gordon shook his head. Julie tried to calm herself. "I know you're going through a lot lately, but that's no excuse."

"Now, hold on a minute, Julie," Dad said quietly.

Julie turned to Pirate Pete and pointed to Gordon. "Tell me, how much did he sell Lucy for?"

"Sell her? Goodness no—we don't just buy any pigeon off the street," said Pirate Pete. "This bird showed up late yesterday afternoon at the fruit stand next door."

Julie paused, confused. "She . . . showed up?"

"That's right," said Pete. "Frank—that's the fruit seller—comes over, and he says to me, 'One of your birds escaped, and it's eating all my bananas!' So I go over there and see this bird chowing down on the fruit, only I see right away that she's not one of mine. But I had an extra cage, so I figured I could give her some food and shelter for a couple of days until I located her owner."

Julie looked at Gordon, unsure what to say.

Gordon spoke softly. "Will you let me explain now?"

Julie nodded, not wanting to say anything else foolish.

"Well, your dad called my mom a little while ago and asked if we could come over. When we arrived, he told us everything that you had told him last night. But you got it all wrong, Julie."

"Then how did you know Lucy was here?"

Dad piped up, "While Gordon was explaining his side of the story, the Humane Society called to tell us that Pirate Pete had found Lucy and was keeping her at his store. We came over right away."

"You called the Humane Society?" Julie asked Pete.

"I was on the phone with them when you came in."

Julie's face turned hot with shame as she realized how wrong she had been about her friend. "I'm so sorry for distrusting you, Gordon. I did get everything wrong, didn't I?"

Mrs. Marino stepped forward. "Not everything, Julie. You were right that Gordon couldn't afford that jacket without a little help."

Gordon looked at his shoes. "I got the money for the jacket from my dad, but I didn't want my mom to know because I didn't want to end up in the middle of another fight between my parents."

Mrs. Marino put her arm around her son. "And here's where I owe you an apology, Gordon. I know how hard you were working to save up your allowance for your jacket, and I think I was a little too tough on you. I shouldn't have been pulling you into the middle of your parents' troubles. Your father and I will both try to do better, I promise."

Pete cleared his throat. "I'll go get Lucy." He

turned to fetch the parrot from the storeroom.

Julie felt limp with relief. Gordon and his mom were getting along, and Gordon had nothing to do with Lucy's disappearance. And best of all, they had found Lucy safe and sound. She couldn't wait to go home and call Ivy.

Yet something was nagging at the back of her mind. "I still have one big question," she said. "If Gordon didn't steal Lucy, and neither Maia nor Mr. Shackley released her, how did Lucy get out?"

Julie looked from face to face, but nobody seemed to have an answer.

14
THE ESCAPE ARTIST

When Pirate Pete returned to the front of the shop with Lucy in a small cage, Julie and Gordon cheered.

"Hi, Lucy," said Gordon. He flapped his elbows.

"Cock-a-doodle-doo!" Lucy crowed, and the whole group laughed.

"That's some bird you've got there, Julie," Pete said. "But have you ever considered investing in one of these?" He wiggled the padlock on the cage door.

"Actually, she's not my parrot. My best friend's family hired me to take care of Lucy this week while they went on vacation."

"Well, you might want to let them know they have quite an escape artist on their hands.

Before I closed the shop last night, I found her flying around the store and riling up the other birds. Take a look at the door on this cage—she chewed it to bits. I had to put this padlock on her cage to keep her from escaping again."

Escape artist? Julie inspected the damaged metal on the cage door. Where had she seen marks like these before? An image flashed into her mind—the nicks on the clip Julie had found lying on the floor beneath Lucy's cage. She gasped. "I think I know what happened: Lucy let herself out!"

"That's certainly possible, Julie," said Maia. "But then how did she open the bedroom door *and* the window?"

Gordon blushed and looked apologetic. "I can answer one of those questions," he said. "The other day, when I went back upstairs to get my jacket, I think I forgot to close the bedroom door when I came back down."

"But you're sure you didn't open the window?" Julie asked.

"Yes, I'm sure," said Gordon. "And I

remember you closing and locking it, Julie."

"So then, who opened the window?" asked Maia.

Once again, nobody had an answer.

Pirate Pete pulled a small key from his pocket and handed it to Julie. "Just to be safe, why don't you put that padlock on her cage at home. You never know when something might set her off and she'll try to escape again."

Julie took the key. "Thank you for taking care of Lucy, Pirate Pete. She's very lucky to have flown into the hands of someone who could help her. And my friend's family will be so happy that she's been found and she's okay."

Mr. Albright handed over a few dollars for the lock and shook Pirate Pete's hand before lifting the small cage off the counter. "We'll be sure to bring back your cage later."

Pirate Pete gave Julie a wink. "Come visit anytime."

Julie, Maia, Gordon, and Mrs. Marino piled into Dad's car for the short ride home, with Julie holding the birdcage on her lap. At Dad's house,

Julie darted in to grab the macramé key chain, and then they all crossed the street to the Lings' house. Once everybody had gathered inside Andrew's room, Gordon was careful to shut the door behind him.

Julie unlocked the padlock and reached into the small cage, inviting the parrot to step onto her wrist. "Here we go, Lucy. Home sweet home," she said, placing her on the perch inside the big cage. "And here's a little homecoming treat!" She peeled a banana, broke it into chunks, and put the pieces on the plate inside the cage before closing the cage door and snapping the padlock shut.

Lucy ate voraciously, her breast pumping as she swallowed each bite.

Maia watched, smiling. "Lucy must have looked so funny standing on top of that pile of bananas at the fruit stand, eating away as if she was in paradise."

Lucy stopped eating and did her siren impression, wailing to everyone's amusement.

They heard a knock on Andrew's door, and in

came Mr. Shackley with his frail wife right behind him. "Is that Lucy we hear?" asked Mr. Shackley.

"Welcome home, Lucy!" said Mrs. Shackley, beaming in the doorway.

Mr. Shackley smiled at Julie. "Our little sleuth has solved the mystery, then?"

Julie grinned. "Well, almost."

Just then, Julie saw Wonton, the orange cat, jump onto the windowsill, purring in the warm sunlight.

Lucy flapped her wings and growled. "Silly cat! Silly cat!" she squawked and then reached her beak through the wire bars to chew at the padlock. Wonton ignored the commotion and rubbed her face against the latch on the window frame. The window popped open.

Julie scooped up the cat and turned to everyone in the room. "Did you see that? The cat just opened the window!" She shooed Wonton out of the room and closed the door. "Here's what must have happened the day Lucy disappeared: after Gordon and I left the house, one of the cats wandered into Andrew's bedroom."

"Through the door that I left open," Gordon mumbled sheepishly.

"Right," Julie said, smiling. "The cat jumped onto the windowsill—Ivy told me the cats love to sun themselves there—and then she rubbed against the latch, opening the window, just the way Wonton did a moment ago. Lucy heard the cat in the room, and she got frightened. She used her beak to open her cage, pulled off the sheet, and flew out the window to escape danger."

"Mystery solved!" Maia announced, and everyone burst into applause.

15
REUNITED

In the morning on Saturday, her last day at Dad's, Julie went over to the Lings' to feed Lucy, Wonton, and Jasmine one last time. "Ivy and her family are coming home today," she told the purring cats as she filled their food and water bowls. Then she went into Andrew's room, closing the door behind her.

"Hey, Alley-oop!" said Lucy as Julie removed the sheet.

"Hey there, Lucy," Julie replied. As she broke up a banana and placed it on the plate in the cage, Julie wondered whether she would ever see Lucy again after today. Julie wasn't sure what time Ivy's family would get home; she hoped she'd have a chance to see Ivy before she left Dad's house and returned to her mom's. Julie sighed. "I'll miss you, Lucy," she said, tapping on the cage. "Don't you give Uncle Lee any trouble, okay?" Lucy shimmied across her perch.

Julie went downstairs and knocked on the pocket door but was disappointed when no one answered. She hoped she'd get a chance to say good-bye to the Shackleys before she returned to Mom's apartment.

Back at Dad's, she rounded up Maia and Dad in the foyer. "There's somewhere special I'd like to take you today," Julie told them. "Come with me." Julie led them down Columbus Avenue and across Washington Square Park. First she introduced them to the newspaper vendor, who was happy to hear that Lucy had been found. Then she took Dad and Maia up Telegraph Hill, to a tree below Coit Tower.

She reached into her pocket and drew out a handful of Lucy's seeds. She tossed them to the ground and watched Maia grin as the flock of green parakeets fluttered around them.

"What a treat!" Maia said, pulling Julie into a hug. "Thank you, Julie."

After dinner, Julie, Maia, and Dad settled into the living room for a game of cards. Julie fetched the big glass jar full of sand dollars and limpet shells that she and Tracy had gathered on trips to the beach. As the story was told in the Albright family, little Julie had once thought sand dollars were real money. Ever since, when she and her father battled at poker, they played with shells instead of chips.

"We've had quite a week," Dad said, distributing the shells in three piles.

"We sure have," said Maia, shuffling the card deck. "You were right, Dan. I've already learned so much in my first few waitressing shifts. And last night, as we were closing up, the chef offered to give me some time in the kitchen on days when the restaurant is slow so that he can teach me a few things."

"That's great, Mary—er—Maia," said Dad.

The phone rang. "I'll get it," Julie called. She dashed to the kitchen and answered.

"Hey, Alley-oop," said Ivy.

"Ivy! Are you home?"

"Yep! We had a fantastic trip, but it's great to be back. Will you and your dad come over? We have a special surprise for you."

"Be there soon!" Julie summoned Maia and Dad, and they walked over to Ivy's house. When they walked in, Julie was surprised to find the pocket door open. She peered in and found the entire Ling family and the Shackleys waiting for her. They burst into applause, and Ivy threw her arms around Julie.

Uncle Lee stepped out from the kitchen with Lucy on his shoulder and carrying a large piece of cake with fancy white frosting. A pretty young woman walked behind him.

"Whose birthday is it?" Julie whispered to Ivy.

"It's nobody's birthday, silly. The cake's for you. Uncle Lee wanted you to have some of his wedding cake."

"For me?"

Uncle Lee set the cake down on the coffee

table and shook her hand. "Ivy and Mr. Shackley explained everything you did for us this week." Then he turned to the woman standing next to him. "Hannah," he said to his new wife, "here's the girl who rescued our Lucy."

Hannah put her hand to her chest and smiled. "It's wonderful to meet you, Julie. How can we ever show our gratitude?"

"Seeing Lucy happy and safe is good enough for me," said Julie.

Mr. Shackley stepped forward. "My wife and I also want to thank you—for bringing some excitement into our lives."

Julie smiled. "I think you'll have to thank Lucy for that," she said. "I hope you'll stop by the neighborhood if you ever decide to come back to San Francisco."

Mr. Shackley nodded. "This city wasn't so bad after all—once I got used to it." He put his arm around his wife.

Uncle Lee looked up at the bird on his shoulder. "I think there's someone else who wants to thank you. Don't you, Lucy?"

Lucy bobbed up and down and screeched, "Ahoy, matey!"

Julie giggled, but Uncle Lee shook his head. "She was supposed to say 'you're my hero!'"

Everyone laughed, and Lucy sang, "Call Roto-Rooter, that's the name. And away go troubles down the drain!"

LOOKING BACK

A PEEK INTO THE PAST

Alex the African Grey parrot shows off his counting skills.

African Grey parrots like Lucy have long
been prized for their high intelligence and
especially for their ability to speak. Scientist
Irene Pepperberg spent 30 years studying her

African Grey,
Alex, who learned
to speak more
than 100 English
words, to count,
and to recognize

Dr. Irene Pepperberg with Alex

colors and shapes. Research on Alex and other birds has provided new insights into the abilities of animal minds—and has given new meaning to the phrase "bird brain"!

A flock of wild African Grey parrots fly in a national park in the Central African Republic.

In Julie's time, parrots were sometimes captured in tropical forests and then sold as pets. Julie would be pleased to know that since 1992, the Wild Bird Conservation Act has banned many wild exotic bird species from being imported into the United States. So today, most exotic bird pets have been hatched and raised in captivity.

Like Lucy and Uncle Lee, captive parrots often form strong bonds with a human companion. But as Julie discovers in the story, although parrots are beautiful and intelligent, they are also

A flock of cherry-headed conures living on Telegraph Hill

noisy and need a lot of attention, and most people are not prepared for the challenges and responsibilities of caring for parrots, who can live for 50 years or more. For these reasons, animal welfare organizations such as the Humane Society do not currently recommend parrots as pets.

While Lucy was happy to reunite with Uncle Lee, who took good care of her, some exotic birds

who escape end up living on their own. Since the early 20th

Coit Tower looms over Telegraph Hill.

This film shows the relationship
between parrots and people
on Telegraph Hill.

century, people have been
telling stories of parrots
living wild on Telegraph Hill
in San Francisco. As Julie
learned, canary-winged parakeets lived on the hill in the
1970s, and since the 1990s, a
large flock of cherry-headed
conures have made the hill's
many trees their home.

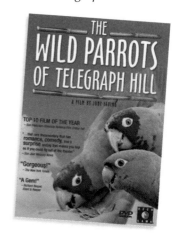

*This film shows the relationship
between parrots and people
on Telegraph Hill.*

Although San Francisco has
colder winters than the birds' native Ecuador
and Peru, the city's weather is still mild enough
to provide food for them year round, and the
flock has more than doubled in size.

In the 1970s, animal lovers like Julie and
Maia helped bring public attention to animal
welfare, including the need to assist lost or
abandoned pets. In 1970, Grace Handley and
her daughter, Virginia, founded the Animal
Switchboard, which Julie calls while searching
for Lucy. For 20 years, Grace and Virginia took
phone calls at all hours of the day and night,

providing support for people who were worried about an animal or pet. San Francisco volunteers continue to run the Animal Switchboard today.

The increased awareness of animal welfare, along with a heightened interest in living a healthy lifestyle and caring for the planet, led to renewed interest in vegetarian eating in the 1970s. Some Americans viewed vegetarianism as an extreme step to take—and it did not help that some vegetarian dishes seemed

These popular books changed the way people thought about food.

The Moosewood Restaurant in Ithaca, New York, is well-known for its creative vegetarian dishes.

strange and unappetizing! But as vegetarian restaurants and cookbooks became popular, people discovered that meatless eating could be not only healthy but tasty, too.

Nowadays, vegetarianism has become a common choice, and the health benefits of eating less meat and more grains, beans, fruits, and vegetables are widely recognized. Today most restaurants usually offer at least one vegetarian option, and the food is just as delicious as anything else on the menu!

About the Author

As a kid, Kathleen O'Dell had fun hanging out in the kitchen with Pete, her great aunt's parakeet. Pete sang commercial jingles from the radio. His favorite was a song about a taxi company that ended with a honking horn!

Kathleen O'Dell is a frequent contributor to *American Girl* magazine and has written many books for girls. She lives in southern California with her husband, Tim, their son, Charlie, and a pug named Max.